SIDDHARTHA

SIDDHARTHA

A NEW TRANSLATION

Hermann Hesse

TRANSLATED BY
Sherab Chödzin Kohn

WITH AN INTRODUCTION BY
Paul W. Morris

SHAMBHALA
Boston & London
2005

SHAMBHALA PUBLICATIONS, INC.
Horticultural Hall
300 Massachusetts Avenue
Boston, Massachusetts 02115
www.shambhala.com

9 8 7 6 5 4 3

PRINTED IN THE UNITED STATES OF AMERICA
Distributed in the United States by Random House, Inc.,
and in Canada by Random House of Canada Ltd

First Mass Market Edition: January 2005
ISBN-13 978-1-59030-227-9
ISBN-10 1-59030-227-3

CONTENTS

TRANSLATOR'S PREFACE

A T THE TIME Hermann Hesse was composing his famous short novel *Siddhartha*, around 1920, he wrote the following words:

> We are seeing a religious wave rising in almost all of Europe, a wave of religious need and despair, a searching and a profound malaise, and many are speaking of . . . a new religion to come. . . . Europe is beginning to sense . . . that the overblown one-sidedness of its intellectual culture (most clearly expressed in scientific specialization) is in need of a correction, a revitalization coming from the opposite pole. This widespread yearning is not for a new ethics or a new way of thinking, but for a culture of the spiritual function that our intellectual approach to life has not been able to provide. This is a general yearning not so much for a Buddha or a Laotze but for a yogic capability. We have learned that humanity can cultivate its intellect to an astonishing level of accomplishment without becoming master of its soul.[1]

These passages sound the call for a sort of "journey to the East," to which *Siddhartha* is the answer. The present-day reader, encountering them undated, might be inclined to place them in a more recent time, in the 1960s and 1970s, when perceptions similar to those described became the germ of a major countercultural groundswell. *Siddhartha* spoke to the seekers of those decades; the novella was in great vogue then.

In fact, pangs of spiritual loss and the desire to cure them by means of "a journey to the East" have seized us recurrently since science and technology—and especially their shocking large-scale manifestation in World War I—seriously began shaking the West's perennial culture. Over the last forty years, in the train of the spiritual shake-up of the sixties and seventies, we have seen the rise of many sorts of "yogic" culture in our society. In the end, it was the East that journeyed to the West. Indian, Tibetan, and Japanese spiritual teachers in particular exerted themselves to transplant their meditative traditions to this hemisphere. This movement had a broad influence on Western societies and the images with which they inspire and entertain themselves, but on the whole its impact has been shallow. "Yogic" insights have petered out into the vague and diluted phenomena of the New Age, and this has now largely run out of energy. Of late, we see life and vitality pouring on a grand scale into a new endemic rapture, the headlong intoxication with new communication technologies and the prosperity they have engendered. More and more American high schools and elementary schools now boast voluntary extra-curricular clubs of avid Internet-wise students of the stock market. Young people of both sexes in large numbers are identifying with cell-phone-and-laptop-toting traders and businesspeople who represent the ultimate cool in a coming world of electronic super-communication. I have seen fourteen-year-old boys going to business meetings in suits.

This new fertility dance with the microchip and the genome is wondrous and colorful beyond words. It is making true a future of which the last century only dreamed. Yet the chances of its expunging or rendering irrelevant the yearning of which Hesse spoke are small; in fact as the materialistic romp reaches extremity, it must surely provoke a further acute outbreak of spirituality. If the yearning for spiritual awakening is an inalienable part of the human spirit, how could it be otherwise?

Thus Hesse's brilliant offering to the human spirit, the spiritual journey of Siddhartha, the brahmin's son, cannot really go out of style. True, Hesse's grasp of Buddhist thinking was imprecise. He did not escape touches of theism and thoughts of sin, being the off-spring, as he was, of two generations of Christian missionaries. Doctrinally, *Siddhartha* is not sharp, but sweetly and naively eclectic. But this hardly matters, for in *Siddhartha*, Hesse captured the truth of the spiritual journey.

Hesse began with a stereotypic, perhaps even corny paradigm. His style was archaic, recalling scripture; he was dealing with a legendary scenario, beyond time, larger than life. But as he proceeded to develop his formula, the story became increasingly real, desperately real—too real for Hesse. His insights cost him heavily. He suffered a major depression and had to stop writing *Siddhartha* for more than a year. His exploration had uncovered a process in which layer after layer of conventional and conceptual reference points have to be stripped away; through inspiration, but also profound disappointment and loss, the seeker relentlessly approaches naked mind. First to come and go for *Siddhartha* is orthodox religion. This is supplanted by life-denying asceticism, which in turn proves inauthentic and has to be given up. The next patch that will not hold is affirmation of self and enjoyment of sensuality and the material world; next, rejection of that approach proves groundless too. At last, understanding at all, any analysis or intellectual grasp, shows itself as ludicrous one-upsmanship in the face of reality's flow; the brilliant seeker's last rag has to be surrendered. The process culminates in the final heartbreaking loss of the spiritual project altogether. Seeking is exhausted at its root and confusion with it. Hesse does not quite give us the "return to the market place" found in the last of the ten Zen Ox-Herding Pictures,[2] but the utter excoriation of ego—all one's world of hopes and fears—is vivid enough. As is the desolate fulfillment inseparable from the seeker's final forlornness. There is total dignity and freedom, surety and cosmic correctness, in not having to attend one's own funeral.

This is where buddhas begin.

Boulder, Colorado
March 2000

NOTES

1. Hermann Hesse, "Die Reden Budhas," in *Aus Indien* (Suhrkamp, 1980), pp. 232–237; translation mine.

2. A series of ten pictures, well-known in the Zen tradition, depicts the stages of the path to enlightenment. The process begins with a man searching for an ox, symbolizing the practitioner trying to get a handle on his awareness. After a long time the man finds the ox's footprints, next he glimpses the animal, finally catches it, tames it, and is able to ride it home. Since the practitioner has now at last become one with his awareness, in the seventh picture the ox disappears; in the eighth the man disappears (ego is gone), and the picture is empty. In the ninth, emptiness disappears—again there are phenomena, appearing brilliant and clear without the projections of ego. In the tenth picture, the man reappears, a nondescript old fellow heading for the marketplace on foot; he drinks at the sake shop, he bargains, he gossips, and whomever encounters him experiences awakening.

INTRODUCTION

BY PAUL W. MORRIS

*I have not only occasionally made a confession
of belief in essays, but once, a little more than
ten years ago, attempted to set forth my belief
in a book. This book is called* Siddhartha.

—HERMANN HESSE, "My Belief," 1931

WHEN NEW DIRECTIONS decided to publish the
first English translation of Hermann Hesse's
Siddhartha in 1951, it could not have foreseen the enormous impact it would have on American culture. The
novel's ostensibly simple narrative—the story of a
young, accomplished brahmin, Siddhartha, who defies
his father's tradition in favor of wandering India
in search of enlightenment—appealed to the restless
drifter, the alienated youth, and the political anarchist
alike. Its many motifs include the outcast from society,
rejection of authority, communion with nature, recal-
citrance toward schooling, and the idea of an imma-
nent God. Published in the United States during the
Cold War, *Siddhartha* addressed a perennial unrest and

provided a new set of values for a generation of young people disenchanted with their parents' conservatism.

By Hesse's own admission, *Siddhartha* is a Western tale cloaked in "Indian garb." The author had chosen India as his backdrop since he was unable to address the concept of an all-pervading unity within the context of his own European Protestant heritage. But Hesse's portrayal of India is based less on his own travels to the subcontinent and more on an imagined notion of "the Orient" so prevalent in Europe during the time of the novel's composition. Like the Romantics and Transcendentalists who had preceded him, Hesse was not interested in accurately conveying the traditions that inspired him. (Hesse's use of the invented term *Yogaveda*, for example, is evidence of his loose rendering of Hinduism.) Instead, he created his own exotic blend of Eastern spirituality that was a synthesis of Hinduism, Buddhism, and Taoism, combined with his burgeoning knowledge of Western psychoanalysis. All this was punctuated with a staunch nonconformity that resonated with readers across both generations and cultures.

Despite Hesse's eclectic interest in the world's religions, no other spiritual discipline—apart from Christianity—permeated his life and work more than Buddhism. Many of his novels were infused with its compassionate foundation, while his characters became centered through developing an awareness of themselves and their own behavior with a kind of mindfulness that transcended the intellectual content of Buddhist philosophy. The author was struck by the Buddha's "life as lived, as labor accomplished and action carried out. A training, a spiritual self-training of the highest order." It is this discipline that we see reflected in Hesse's writing and in his own psychological struggle.

His most influential work, *Siddhartha* is arguably also his most optimistic. The novel offered its readers hope for liberation in this lifetime, a hope that was absent from both the German and the American youth movements that had surfaced in the wake of two world wars. There could not have been a more encouraging message available to those who sought the "Way Within." As a result, America witnessed a Hesse phenomenon that was unparalleled for a European writer. And yet, despite its seemingly preordained success in America, the odds seemed stacked against the novel ever being finished in the first place. It was only through a series of transformative experiences, wherein the author reinvented himself, that *Siddhartha* was born. Indeed, the novel had a journey all its own prior to its arrival on American soil; the author's process of self-realization was inextricably tied to the composition of the novel itself.

In 1918, a year and a half before he would begin work on his Indian legend, Hermann Hesse awoke from a dream one rainy morning in Berne, Switzerland. He lay motionless in a quasi-dream state, not yet awake enough to look at his clock, and slowly ascended from layers of sleep to become aware of his surroundings. His head ached as he looked around his room, noticing the way the light fell on his clothes draped over a chair, the play of shapes concealed in the mist that rolled past his window. He longed to fall back to sleep, but as he heard the rain falling softly on the roof, he was filled with great sadness and pain; the memory of a long dream had emerged with him from his slumber like a shadow. Hesse would later relate the dream in his diary—how he had heard two voices, both of which spoke to him of a profound sorrow, but it was the second voice, the deeper and more resonant of the two, that commanded: "Listen to me! Listen to me, and remember: suffering is nothing, suffering is illusion. Only you yourself create it, only you cause yourself pain!"

After contemplating the dream's meaning, he described the second voice, saying it "was itself dark, it was itself primal cause." That Hesse should dwell so intently on a dream is no surprise: As early as 1916, following the second of several nervous breakdowns, he had undergone psychoanalysis with a therapist and disciple of Carl G. Jung (and would benefit later from analysis with the prominent psychologist himself). Hesse was well acquainted with Jung's notion that the unconscious could access wisdom available to the whole of humanity. He knew that this voice was a response to the fundamental question of existence that had been hounding him since childhood.

Until then, Hesse's entire life had been a series of

rebellions, from his dropping out of school at the age of thirteen, to his break with the tradition of his Protestant parents and their hope that he follow their missionary ambitions, to his fierce opposition to the global conflict of World War I. His grandfather, who was proficient in nine Indian languages and who was widely acknowledged throughout Europe as an authority on the subcontinent, encouraged the young Hesse's appreciation for the spiritual classics, which led to the author's realization "that not only East and West, not only Europe and Asia are unities, but that there is a unity and an association over and beyond that—humanity." It was his grandfather's love of India that convinced Hesse, a decade after his mentor's death, to travel there in 1911 in an attempt to reconcile his family's missionary tradition with his own rebellious spirit. His exposure to Indic culture, and to Buddhism in particular, would color much of his later work, but the experience of his journey to the East did not satisfy his spiritual longing.

In 1919 Hesse sought solace and escaped to Montagnola, a town in the foothills of the southern Swiss Alps, a small village where he would reside for the rest of his life. Although his colleagues teased him that he had become a monk, Hesse felt he had finally succeeded in achieving what he had yearned for years earlier when, at the height of his restlessness as a husband and father, he had proclaimed: "I would give my left hand if I could again be a poor happy bachelor and own nothing but twenty books, a second pair of boots, and a box full of secretly composed poems." However, his newfound independence had a greater price than mere corporeal sacrifice: Forced to commit his wife to an asylum after her rapid descent into schizophrenia, he was unable to provide for his three sons and regretfully placed them in the care of friends. It is clear from his correspondence during this year that both decisions weighed heavily upon his conscience. Yet, despite the emotional stress, Hesse emerged from his own period of crisis—during which time World War I had ended—to experience one of the most productive and creative years of his life. This significant shift in perspective was most evident in December 1919, when Hesse began composing *Siddhartha*. The writing came easily to him at first, and he completed Part One in the early months of 1920. Then, nothing.

Despondent, he wrote to a friend in mid-1920: "For many months my Indian 'poem,' my falcon, my sunflower, the hero of Siddhartha, lies fallow." Unable to further advance the novel, he confessed to another friend that "my big Indian work isn't ready yet and may never be. I'm setting it aside for now, because I would have to depict a next phase of development that I have not yet fully experienced myself." This statement reveals the severity of Hesse's existential plight. The initial chapters that comprise Part One are concerned with Siddhartha's unrest; his questioning mind; and his refusal to follow the brahmanical tradition of his father, the mendicant path of the wandering ascetic, and even the contemplative way of the Buddha. These chapters had, according to Hesse, "proceeded splendidly," informed by the author's own questioning mind. But in order for Part Two to be successful, Hesse would have to contend with the protagonist's triumph, whereby Siddhartha finally attains enlightenment. Conceiving such a solution to his character's suffering was impossible, however, as long as the author remained disassociated from his own inner being.

If not for Hesse's unrelenting determination for self-discovery, *Siddhartha* surely would have been abandoned. In July 1921, this might have seemed to be the case when Part One was published independently without a proper ending. Through his close work with Jung during these years, Hesse confronted his dislocation from society to complete his own journey while *Siddhartha* remained adrift. With Jung, Hesse revisited his childhood, a childhood filled with Indian antiquities set against the backdrop of Christian iconography. He re-immersed himself in the world's sacred literature that he had first encountered as a child in his grandfather's library. And he discovered an appreciation for the teachings of the Buddha. Of course, Hesse's sympathy for Buddhism was not solely responsible for his eventual catharsis; Buddhist thought had been just one component of his general awareness of the Asian religions that were in vogue at that time. But the influence that the Buddha's teachings had on the writing of *Siddhartha* is unmistakable. Early in 1921, Hesse wrote to an artist friend of how Buddhism had been his "sole source of consolation" for years, and although he admitted that "gradually my attitude changed, and I'm no longer a Buddhist," he acknowledged the benefits of Buddhist practice later that year:

> The point and goal of meditation is not knowledge in the sense of our Western intellectuality but an alteration of consciousness, a technique whose highest result is pure harmony, a simultaneous and equal cooperation of logical intuitive thinking.

As he grew more familiar with Buddhist doctrine, Hesse began to understand the subtleties of practice that moved him out of his acute depression. For him, the speeches of the Buddha were "a source and mine of quite unparalleled richness and depth," he wrote in his diary. He continued:

> As soon as we cease to regard Buddha's teaching simply intellectually and acquiesce with a certain sympathy in the age-old Eastern concept of unity, if we allow Buddha to speak to us as vision, as image, as the awakened one, the perfect one, we find in him, almost independently of the philosophic content and dogmatic kernel of his teaching, a great prototype of mankind. Whoever attentively reads a small number of the countless "speeches" of Buddha is soon aware of a harmony in them, a quietude of soul, a smiling transcendence, a totally unshakable firmness, but also invariable kindness, endless patience.

Resuming work on the novel in early 1922, he quickly completed the eight chapters that comprise Part Two.

By May of that year the novel was finished. Hesse's *Siddhartha*—whose name in Sanskrit means "he who has found the goal"—comes to rest in a middle way just as Hesse himself discovers his own way out of depression. The author's understanding of Buddhism has its finest expression toward the end of the novel, when Siddhartha quietly meditates on the movement of the river: "He had died and a new Siddhartha had awakened from his sleep. He too would grow old and would have to die. Siddhartha was impermanent, every formed thing was impermanent." Finally, in October of 1922, the novel was published in its entirety.

Hesse was not completely satisfied with the finished work. In a letter to a colleague he expressed doubt that he had "reformulated for our era a meditative Indian ideal of how to live one's life." But a few months before the novel's publication, an Indian professor from Calcutta who had seen the finished work impressed upon the author the imperative that *Siddhartha* "be translated in all European languages, for here we face for the first time the real East presented to the West." Encouraged, Hesse wrote to a friend expressing his hope that the novel appear in English, "not for the sake of the English themselves but for those Asians and others whom it would vindicate."

As early as 1925, the first translation into Japanese appeared, followed later by editions into many Indian languages during the fifties. And though a Chinese translation did not appear until 1968, the enormous demand in Asia for this imaginative Indian tale is testament to the universal truth that Hesse had apprehended. Contented with the reception of his lyrical novel, Hesse never returned to India as a literary device, but his appreciation for the Buddha's teachings did not wane.

Hesse said of sacred literature: "The very oldest works age the least." This sentiment may be applied to *Siddhartha* as well, for it is as fresh as ever, still relevant today as it was in the 1920s in Germany and in the 1960s in America. The novel has journeyed through a century of turmoil bearing witness to human suffering. A year before his death in 1962, while *Siddhartha* climbed to commercial success in the United States, the author described how one of the "simple and immediately impressive" Zen koans struck him as a revelation: "[It] overcame me like a breath from the universe, I experienced an ecstasy and at the same time a terror as in those rare moments of immediate awareness of experience which I call 'awakening.'" Similarly, *Siddhartha* served in koan-like fashion to wake millions from their delusions, to inspire, challenge, and remind, as Hesse's dream-voice had done, that "suffering is nothing, suffering is illusion."

BIBLIOGRAPHY

Freedman, Ralph. *Hermann Hesse, Pilgrim of a Crisis: A Biography.* New York: Fromm International, 1997.

Hesse, Hermann. *Autobiographical Writings.* Edited by Theodore Ziolkowski, translated by Denver Lindley. New York: Farrar, Straus & Giroux, 1972.

Hesse, Hermann. *My Belief: Essays on Life and Art.* Edited by Theodore Ziolkowski, translated by Denver Lindley. New York: Farrar, Straus & Giroux, 1974.

Hesse, Hermann. *Soul of the Age: Selected Letters of Hermann Hesse, 1891–1962.* Edited by Theodore Ziolkowski, translated by Mark Harman. New York: Farrar, Straus & Giroux, 1991.

Mileck, Joseph. *Hermann Hesse: Life, Work, and Criticism.* Fredericton, N.B., Canada: York Press, 1984.

Serrano, Miguel. *C.G. Jung and Hermann Hesse: A Record of Two Friendships.* Translated by Frank MacShane. New York: Schocken Books, 1966.

Tusken, Lewis W. *Understanding Hermann Hesse: The Man, His Myth, His Metaphor.* Columbia, S.C.: University of South Carolina Press, 1998.

PART ONE

The Brahmin's Son

IN THE SHADOW of the house, in the sun on the riverbank by the boats, in the shadow of the sal-tree forest, in the shadow of the fig tree, Siddhartha, the beautiful brahmin's son, the young falcon, grew up with his friend, the brahmin's son Govinda. The sun on the riverbank browned his pale shoulders as he bathed, as he performed sacred ablutions, as he performed sacred sacrifices. Shadows flowed in his dark eyes in the mango grove as he played his boy's games, as his mother sang, during the sacred sacrifices, while his father, the scholar, taught, and during the discourses of the wise men. For a long time now Siddhartha had taken part in the discourses of the wise men, training in debate with Govinda, training in the art of contemplation with Govinda, in the practice of meditative absorption. He already knew how to say the OM without sound, the word of words, to speak it soundlessly inward with the in-breath and soundlessly outward with the out-breath, with his mind collected, his brow aglow with the radiance of a clear-thinking intellect. He already knew how to see his being's atman within him, indestructible, one with the universe.

Joy leaped in his father's heart over his brilliant son, so thirsty for knowledge. He saw a great sage and a priest growing in him, a prince among the brahmins. Bliss leaped in his mother's bosom as she watched him— watched him walking, watched him sitting and standing—Siddhartha, the strong, the beautiful, moving with his lithe-limbed walk, greeting her with perfect grace.

Love stirred in the hearts of the young daughters of the brahmins when Siddhartha passed through the city streets, with his radiant brow, with his imperial glance, with his slender hips.

But his friend, the brahmin's son Govinda, loved him more than any other. He loved Siddhartha's gaze and his sweet voice, he loved his way of walking and the complete grace of his movements; he loved everything Siddhartha did and said, but most of all, he loved his mind—his elevated, fiery thoughts, his burning will, his lofty inspiration. Govinda knew Siddhartha would never become an ordinary brahmin, a lazy purveyor of rituals, a greedy dealer in charms, a vain mouther of empty phrases, a base and devious priest, nor would he become a mindless good sheep in the common herd. Certainly he would not; and Govinda, too, would not become any of those things; he also would not become a brahmin like ten thousand others. His desire was to follow Siddhartha, the beloved, the magnificent. And if Siddhartha ever became a god, if he ever entered the light, then Govinda would follow him—as his friend, as his companion, as his servant, his spear bearer, his shadow.

Yes, everyone loved Siddhartha. He aroused joy in everyone, he was a delight to all.

But Siddhartha was no joy to himself; he brought no pleasure to himself. Walking on the rosy paths of the fig garden, sitting in the bluish shadows of the meditation grove, washing his limbs in his daily baths of purification, performing sacrifices in the deep shade of the mango wood, perfect in the grace of his gestures, he was beloved of everyone, a joy to all—but still there was no joy in his heart. Dreams came to him and restless thoughts. They flowed into him from the water of the river, glittered from the night stars, melted out of the rays of the sun. Dreams came and a restless mind, rising in the smoke of the offerings, wafting from the verses of the *Rigveda*, seeping into him from the teachings of the old brahmins.

Siddhartha had begun to breed discontent within himself. He had begun to feel that his father's love and his mother's love, and even the love of his friend Govinda, would not bring him enduring happiness, would not bring him contentment and satisfaction, would not be sufficient to his needs. He had begun to sense that his venerable father and his other teachers, the wise brahmins, had already shared with him the better part of their wisdom; they had already poured their all into his waiting vessel, and the vessel was not full, his mind was not satisfied, his soul was not at peace, his heart was not content.

The ritual ablutions were good, but they were water—they did not wash away sins, they did not heal the mind's thirst, they did not resolve the heart's fear. The sacrifices and the invocations of the gods were splendid, but was this all there was? Did sacrifices bring happiness? And what about the gods? Did Prajapati really create the world? Was it not atman—That, the one and only and the all in all? Were the gods not formed things, created like you and me and subject to time, impermanent? So was it good, a meaningful and supreme act, to sacrifice to the gods? To what other should one make offerings, what other should one worship besides That, the one and only, atman? And where was atman to be found, where did it dwell, where did its eternal heart beat? Where else but in one's own inmost self, the indestructible essence within everyone. But where was this self, this inmost essence, this ultimate principle? It was neither flesh nor bone, neither thought nor consciousness—so the wise men taught. So where was it then? Was there any worthwhile path other than one leading to That, the self, the me, atman? But nobody taught this path! No one acknowledged it—his father did not, nor the teachers and wise men, nor the sacred liturgy. They knew it all, the brahmins and their holy books, knew everything! They had covered everything and more—the creation of the world, the origin of speech, nutrition, the in-breath and the out-breath, the ordering of the senses, the deeds of the gods—their knowledge was endless! But what good did it do to know all these things if one did not know the one and only, the most important thing, the only important thing?

True, many verses in the holy books—the Upanishads, the *Samaveda*—spoke of this inmost and ultimate essence. Glorious verses! "Your soul is the whole
world," it proclaims in those writings; also that in sleep,
deep sleep, a person enters his inmost sanctum and
dwells in the atman. These verses contained marvelous
wisdom—everything in them is the knowledge of the
wisest of the wise formulated in magical words, pure as
bee-gathered honey. No, the immensity of knowledge
that lay preserved there, gathered by countless generations of wise brahmins, should not be underestimated.
But where were the brahmins, the priests, the sages, or
the ascetics who had succeeded not only in knowing this
most profound knowledge intellectually but also in living it? Where were the adepts who had learned the
knack of bringing indwelling in the atman out of the
realm of sleep into that of wakefulness, who had made it
a part of every aspect of life, both word and deed? Siddhartha was acquainted with many venerable brahmins, his father above all. His father was a pure, a
learned, a supremely venerable man, admirable, peace-
ful and noble in demeanor, pure in his life, wise in his
words, refined and elevated in his thought. But even his
father, who knew so much—did he live in holy bliss, and
had he found contentment? Was he, too, not only a
seeker, still thirsting? Did he not have to slake his thirst
again and again at the sacred springs—the rites, the
books, the discourses of the brahmins? Why did he,
blameless as he was, have to wash away his sins each day,
perform purifications each day, each day again? Was

atman not within him? Did the primordial spring not flow in his own heart? That is what had to be found—the primordial spring within one's self; one had to become master of that! Anything else was a vain quest, a false direction, a misunderstanding.

These were Siddhartha's thoughts. This was his thirst and his pain.

He often repeated to himself the words of the *Chandogya Upanishad*: "Verily, the name of Brahman is Satyam; truly he who knows this enters daily into the heavenly realm." Often the heavenly realm seemed near, but he had never attained it completely, never quenched his ultimate thirst. And of all the wise men he knew and whose teaching he enjoyed—even the wisest of the sages—none of them had attained the heavenly realm completely, none had entirely quenched the eternal thirst.

"Govinda," said Siddhartha to his friend, "Govinda, my friend, come with me under the banyan tree, and we shall practice meditation."

They went over to the banyan tree and sat down, Siddhartha in one place and Govinda twenty paces farther on. As he sat down, prepared to utter the OM, Siddhartha murmured this verse:

OM is the bow, the arrow is the soul,
Brahman is the arrow's target.
One should strike it without wavering.

When the customary amount of time for meditation had passed, Govinda got up. Evening had come; it was time to perform the evening ablutions. He called Siddhartha's name. Siddhartha did not reply. Siddhartha was absorbed, his eyes fixed on a very distant goal, his tongue protruding a bit between his teeth. He did not seem to be breathing. He sat, wrapped in absorption, thinking OM, his soul like an arrow flying toward Brahman.

One day some shramanas passed through Siddhartha's city, ascetics on pilgrimage, three gaunt, lifeless men, neither young nor old, with dust-coated, bleeding shoulders, nearly naked, sun-scorched, isolated and solitary, alien and outcast, misfits and scrawny jackals in the world of humans. A fevered atmosphere of silent fervor, wasting privation, and pitiless self-immolation hung over them.

In the evening, after the hour of contemplation, Siddhartha said to Govinda: "Tomorrow morning, my friend, Siddhartha will go to the shramanas. He will become a shramana."

Hearing these words, Govinda paled; he read in his friend's face a resolve as impossible to divert as a bowshot arrow. At once, in this first glimpse, Govinda saw it: It is starting now; now Siddhartha is embarking on his path, now his destiny is taking shape—and with his, mine too! And he became pale as a dried-out banana peel.

"Siddhartha," he cried, "will your father permit this?"

Siddhartha looked over at him like one awakening

from sleep. With an arrow's swiftness, he saw into Govinda's soul and read there both fear and surrender.

"Govinda," he said softly, "let us not waste words. Tomorrow at dawn I begin the life of a shramana. Speak no more about it."

Siddhartha entered the room where his father was seated on a hemp mat. He moved up behind his father and stood there until his father felt there was somebody behind him. "Is that you, Siddhartha?" said the brahmin.

Siddhartha said, "With your permission, Father, I've come to tell you that tomorrow I must leave your house and go off with the ascetics. I long to become a shramana. May my father not oppose this."

The brahmin was silent and remained so for so long that the stars moved and changed their configuration in the little window in the room before the silence came to an end. The son stood mute and motionless, his arms crossed; the father sat mute and motionless on the mat, and the stars moved in the sky. Finally the father said: "It is not fitting for a brahmin to speak hard and angry words, yet in my heart I cannot accept this. Do not let this request cross your lips a second time."

The brahmin got slowly to his feet. Siddhartha remained standing there with his arms crossed.

"What are you waiting for?" said his father.

"You know," said Siddhartha.

Upset, his father left the room and went and lay down on his bed.

After an hour, since sleep did not come, the brahmin

got up and began to pace back and forth. He stepped out of the house and looked in through the little window of the room. He saw Siddhartha standing there with crossed arms, still not having moved. His light-colored upper robe shone pale. With apprehension in his heart, the father returned to his bed.

After an hour, since sleep did not come to him, the brahmin got up again, paced back and forth, stepped out in front of the house, and saw that the moon had risen. He glanced in through the window. There stood Siddhartha motionless, his arms crossed, with the moonlight playing on his bare shins. Troubled in his heart, the father went back to his bed.

And he came back after one hour and again after two hours, looked through the little window, and saw Siddhartha standing there, in the moonlight, in the starlight, in the darkness. And came back again, hour after hour, and looked without speaking into the room, saw the unmoving figure standing, and his heart filled with anger, filled with concern, filled with uncertainty, filled with pain.

And the last hour of the night, before day broke, he came back again, went into the room, and looked at the youth standing there. The boy looked big to him and alien.

"Siddhartha," he said, "what are you waiting for?"

"You know."

"Are you going to keep standing there, till daylight, till noon, till night?"

"I'm going to stand here and wait."

"You'll get tired, Siddhartha."

"I'll get tired."

"You'll fall asleep, Siddhartha."

"I will not fall asleep."

"You'll die, Siddhartha."

"I will die."

"And would you rather die than obey your father?"

"Siddhartha has always obeyed his father."

"So will you give up your idea?"

"Siddhartha will do what his father tells him."

The first daylight shone into the room. The brahmin saw that Siddhartha's knees were shaking slightly. But he saw no wavering in Siddhartha's face. The eyes were fixed on the distance. Then the father realized that Siddhartha was already no longer home with him, that he had left him already.

The father laid his hand on Siddhartha's shoulder.

"You will go off to the forest," he said, "and become a shramana. If you find happiness in the forest, come back and teach me happiness. If it's disappointment you find, then come back and we shall again make sacrifices to the gods together. Now go and kiss your mother, and tell her where you're going. For me, it's time to go to the river and perform the first ablutions."

He took his hand from his son's shoulder and went out. Siddhartha tottered sideways as he tried to take a step. He forced his legs to obey him, bowed to his father, and went to find his mother, so he could do as his father had told him.

As the wayfarer was leaving the quiet city by first

light, walking slowly on stiff legs, a shadow emerged from behind the last house, where it had been crouching, and joined him. It was Govinda.

"You came," said Siddhartha and smiled.

"I came," said Govinda.

With the Shramanas

O N THE EVENING of the same day, they caught
up with the ascetics, those gaunt shramanas,
and offered to join them and attend them faithfully.
They were accepted.

Siddhartha gave his robe to a poor brahmin he met
on the road. Now he wore only a loincloth and an un-
stitched, earth-colored shawl. He ate only once a day
and never cooked food. He fasted for fifteen days. He
fasted for twenty-eight days. The flesh fell away from
his cheeks and thighs. Fevered dreams flashed from
his dilated eyes, the nails got long on his shriveled
fingers, and from his chin grew a dry, scruffy beard.
His eyes became hard as iron when he encountered
women. His lip curled with contempt when he walked
through a town among well-dressed people. He saw
merchants bargaining, princes going off to the hunt,
grief-stricken people mourning their dead, prostitutes
offering their bodies, doctors working over the sick,
priests determining the day of sowing, lovers making
love, mothers nursing their babies—and none of it was
worthy of his glance. It was all a lie, it all stank, it was
all putrid with lies. Everything pretended to meaning

14

and happiness and beauty, but it was all only putrescence and decay. The taste of the world was bitter. Life was pain.

Siddhartha had one single goal before him—to become empty, empty of thirst, empty of desire, empty of dreams, empty of joy and sorrow. To die away from himself, no longer to be "I," to find the peace of an empty heart, to be open to wonder within an egoless mind—that was his goal. When every bit of ego was overcome and dead, when in his heart all cravings and compulsions had been stilled, then the ultimate must awaken, that innermost essence in one's being that is no longer ego, the great mystery.

Siddhartha stood silent as the sun blazed straight down upon him, afire with pain, afire with thirst, and kept standing till he no longer felt pain or thirst. Silent he stood during the rainy season, with water dripping from his hair onto his freezing shoulders, onto his freezing hips and legs; and the ascetic kept standing there until his shoulders and limbs were no longer freezing, till they ceased to complain, till they were still. Silent he squatted in the thorn brambles, blood dripping from his burning flesh and pus from his sores; and Siddhartha remained there immobile, not stirring, until his blood no longer ran, until the stinging stopped and the burning was over.

Siddhartha sat erect and learned to hold his breath, learned to make do with only a little breath, learned to stop breathing. He learned, beginning from his breathing, to calm his heartbeat, learned to diminish the beating of his heart until it beat only a few times, hardly at all.

Taught by the eldest shramana, Siddhartha practiced self-abnegation, practiced meditative absorption according to the new instructions of the shramanas. A heron flew over the bamboo grove, and Siddhartha became one with the heron in his mind, flew over forest and mountain, became a heron, ate fish, hungered with a heron's hunger, spoke a heron's croaking language, died a heron's death. There was a dead jackal lying on the sandy bank, and Siddhartha's mind slipped into the carcass, became a dead jackal, lay on the shore, swelled up, stank, rotted, was torn to pieces by hyenas, flayed by vultures, became a skeleton, became dust, blew about in the fields. And Siddhartha's mind returned, dead, rotten, reduced to dust, having tasted the dark drunkenness of the cycle of existence. With a new craving it lay in wait like a hunter for the gap where that cycle could be escaped, where the end of causation could begin, eternity without suffering. He mortified his senses, immolated his memory; he slipped out of his ego into a thousand alien forms, became a beast, carrion, became stone, wood, water—yet each time when he awoke he found himself there again. By sunshine or by moonlight, he was once again ego, was pressed back into the cycle, felt craving, overcame the craving, felt craving anew.

Siddhartha learned a great deal from the shramanas, learned many pathways beyond the self. He followed the path of self-extinction by means of pain, by means of suffering intentionally and overcoming the pain, the hunger, the thirst, the fatigue. He followed the path of self-extinction by means of meditation, allowing the senses to empty themselves of all representations. These and other pathways he learned and followed. A thousand times he left his ego behind; for hours and days at a time he dwelled in nonego. But even if the methods he followed led beyond ego, in the end they led back to ego. Though Siddhartha slipped out of ego's grasp a thousand times, dwelled in nothingness, dwelled in beasts, in stones, the return was inevitable, the moment when he would find himself back again was inescapable. Whether by sunshine or moonlight, in shadow or in rain, once again Siddhartha and ego appeared, and once again he felt the torment of the cycle of existence forced upon him.

Beside him lived Govinda, his shadow, following the same paths, undertaking the same efforts. Seldom did they exchange words beyond what was required by their tasks and their practices. From time to time they went together through the villages to beg food for themselves and their teachers.

"What do you think, Govinda?" said Siddhartha once during one of these begging rounds. "What do you think—have we made any progress? Have we reached any goals?"

Govinda replied: "We've learned and we're still learning. You're going to be a great shramana, Siddhartha. You've learned all the practices very fast; the old shramanas have often expressed admiration for you. You're going to be a saint, O Siddhartha."

Siddhartha said: "That is not the way it looks to me, my friend. What I have learned up to now from the shramanas, O Govinda, I could have learned faster and more simply. I could have learned it, my friend, in any tavern in the whore's quarter, from the teamsters and dice players."

Govinda replied: "Siddhartha is making fun of me. How could you have learned meditative absorption, holding the breath, or indifference to hunger and pain in such a place from those miserable people?"

And Siddhartha said softly, as though speaking to himself: "What is meditative absorption? What is leaving the body? What is fasting? What is holding the breath? These are a flight from the ego, a brief escape from the torment of being an ego, a short-term deadening of the pain and absurdity of life. This same escape, this same momentary deadening, is achieved by the ox driver in an inn when he drinks a bowl of rice wine or fermented coconut milk. Then he no longer feels his self, then he no longer feels the pains of life—he achieves momentary numbness. Falling asleep over his bowl of rice wine, he reaches the same result Siddhartha and Govinda reach when, through long practice sessions, they escape their bodies and dwell in nonego. That is the way it is, Govinda."

Govinda said, "You say that, O friend, but at the same time you know that Siddhartha is no ox driver and shramanas do not tipple. The drunkard does achieve numbness, he does find a brief reprieve and rest, but he comes back from his intoxication and finds everything as it was before and is none the wiser; he has accumulated no knowledge and climbed not one rung higher."

Siddhartha smiled and said: "I do not know. I have never been a drinker. But that through my practice of austerities and meditative absorptions I find only a transitory numbness and remain just as far from wisdom and liberation as when I was a babe in my mother's womb, this I do know, Govinda, this I know."

And another time, as Siddhartha was coming out of the forest with Govinda to beg some food in the village for their fellow ascetics and teachers, Siddhartha began talking again, saying: "How now, Govinda, are we really on the right track? Are we really approaching realization? Are we getting close to attaining liberation? Or are we not going in a circle—we whose intention was to escape the vicious circle of existence?"

Govinda said: "We have learned a great deal, Siddhartha, and there remains a lot more still to learn. We are not going in a circle, we are moving upward. The circle is a spiral; we have already advanced through a number of stages."

Siddhartha replied: "How old do you think our oldest shramana is, our venerable teacher?"

Govinda said: "Our eldest is perhaps sixty years old."

Siddhartha replied: "He has reached sixty and still has not attained nirvana. He will get to be seventy and eighty; and you and I, too, we will get old, and we will do our practices and fast and meditate. But we will not attain nirvana; neither will he. O Govinda, I think that of all the shramanas who exist, there is perhaps not one who will attain nirvana. We find consolation, we find a deadening, we learn skills that we use to deceive ourselves. But we are not finding the essential, the path of paths."

"Would you be so kind," said Govinda, "as to refrain from making such terrible statements, Siddhartha! How is it possible that among so many brahmins, so many strict and venerable shramanas, among so many seekers, so many fervent students, so many holy men, not one of them should find the path of paths?"

But Siddhartha replied in a voice that contained both mockery and sadness, in a soft, somewhat sad, somewhat mocking tone: "Soon, Govinda, your friend will abandon this path of the shramanas in which he has accompanied you for so long. I suffer thirst, O Govinda, and on this long path of a shramana, my thirst has not grown any less. I have always thirsted for understanding; I have always been full of questions. Year after year, I asked questions of the brahmins; year after year, I asked questions of the holy Vedas. Perhaps, O Govinda, it would have been just as good, just as clever, just as meaningful to address my questions to a tickbird or a chimpanzee. I have taken a long time—and I have not yet finished—to learn the following, Govinda: It is impossible to learn anything! In my opinion, that thing that we call 'learning' does not exist. The only thing that exists, my friend, is a knowing that is everywhere, which is atman, which is in me and in you and in every being. And I am beginning to believe that this knowing has no greater enemy than wanting to know, than learning."

Here Govinda stopped on the way and raised his hand, saying: "Siddhartha, kindly refrain from frightening your friend with talk of this sort! Truly your words arouse fear in my heart. Just consider, if everything were as you say and there were no learning, what would become of the sacredness of prayer, of the venerability of brahminhood, of the holiness of the shramanas? Where, Siddhartha, does that leave everything on earth that is sacred, worthy, venerable?"

And Govinda murmured as if to himself a verse from one of the Upanishads:

He who, meditating with pure mind, becomes
    absorbed in the atman—
Inexpressible in words is the bliss of his heart.

But Siddhartha did not reply. He was thinking about the words Govinda had said to him, thinking them through to the end.

Yes, he thought, standing there with his head hanging, what would remain of everything that once seemed sacred to us? What would be left? What would stand the test?

When the two youths had been living with the shramanas and practicing together for about three years, news reached them by various direct and indirect paths, a rumor, a legend: A man named Gotama had appeared—an exalted one, a buddha—who had overcome within himself the suffering of the world and brought the wheel of rebirth to a standstill. It was said that he traveled through the countryside teaching, surrounded by disciples, without possessions, homeless, without women. He wore the yellow robe of an ascetic, but he had a radiant countenance; he was a blessed being, and brahmins and princes bowed down to him and became his disciples.

This legend, this rumor, this fable, was heard here and there, it floated about. In the cities the brahmins talked about it; in the forest haunts of the shramanas, the name of Gotama came to the ears of the youths repeatedly, as something good or something evil, with praise and with calumny.

As when plague is raging in a country and the word goes out that, here or there, there is a man, a wise man, a man of skill, whose word and presence are enough to heal anyone who has fallen prey to the disease, and as when this news spreads through the land and everyone is talking about it, many people believe, many are dubious, but anyway many people set out immediately to find the wise man, the benefactor—in this way the legend spread through the land, the fragrant legend of Gotama the Buddha, the sage of the Shakya tribe. According to believers, he was possessed of supreme knowledge, he remembered his previous lives, had attained nirvana and never returned into the cycle of existence, was never swallowed back into the troubled stream of formations. Many wondrous and incredible things were said of him—he had performed miracles, subdued the devil, spoken with the gods. His enemies and doubters, however, said that this Gotama was no more than a seducer who passed his days in comfort and pleasure, was contemptuous of sacrifices, devoid of scholarly learning, and a stranger to spiritual practices and austerities.

The legend of the Buddha had a sweet sound to it; a magical fragrance arose out of these accounts. The world was ailing, life hard to bear—and lo, here a freshet seemed to spring, a message to sound, consoling, mild, full of promise. Everywhere, wherever the message of the Buddha was heard, throughout the kingdoms of India, youths took heed, felt longing, felt hope, and among the sons of brahmins in the towns and villages, every wayfarer and stranger was welcome who brought word of him, the Exalted One, Shakyamuni.

The legend reached even to the shramanas in the forest, even to Siddhartha and Govinda. Slowly it came to them, drop by drop, each drop heavy with hope, each drop heavy with doubt. They spoke of it little, for the eldest of the shramanas was not well disposed toward this legend. It was his understanding that this supposed buddha had previously been an ascetic and lived in the forest but had then returned to the comfortable life and the pleasures of the world, and he took a dim view of this Gotama.

"Siddhartha," said Govinda one day to his friend, "today I was in the village, and a brahmin invited me into his house; and in his house was a brahmin's son from Magadha who had seen the Buddha with his own eyes and heard him teach. My breath caught in my chest and I thought to myself, 'Couldn't I, too, couldn't both of us, Siddhartha and I, also experience that moment of hearing the teaching from the mouth of that Perfect One?' What do you say, friend, should we not go too and hear the teaching from the mouth of the Buddha?"

Siddhartha replied: "Govinda, I always thought: 'Govinda will remain with the shramanas. I always believed that was his goal—to reach sixty or seventy years of age and still be carrying on with those arts and practices that are the glory of the shramanas. But you see, I didn't know Govinda well enough; how little I knew his heart.' So, my dearest friend, you want to strike out afresh and go to where the Buddha is proclaiming his teaching."

Govinda replied, "You love to mock me. Mock me as much as you like, Siddhartha! But don't you also have a longing to hear this teaching? Has that desire not been aroused in you as well? And did you not once say to me that you would not be following the way of the shramanas much longer?"

Then Siddhartha laughed in his particular way, in which his voice took on a shade of mockery and a shade of sadness, and said: "Well said, Govinda, you have spoken well and remembered rightly. But kindly also remember the other thing you heard from me—that I have become distrustful of doctrines and learning and tired of them—I have little faith in words that come to us from teachers. But very well, my friend, I am willing to hear that teaching, even though in my heart I believe we have already tasted the best of its fruits."

Govinda said: "Your willingness brings joy to my heart. But tell me, how is that possible? How could the best fruits of Gotama's teaching already have been revealed to us before we have even heard it?"

Siddhartha said: "Let us savor this fruit for now and let any others wait, Govinda. For the fruit for which we can already thank Gotama is this: He is summoning us away from the shramanas! Whether he has something more and better to offer us, my friend, let us patiently wait and see."

This same day Siddhartha announced to the eldest shramana his decision to leave him. He announced this to the elder with politeness and humility befitting a pupil and disciple. But the shramana got angry that both youths intended to leave him; he raised his voice and used coarse language.

Govinda was intimidated and embarrassed; but Siddhartha leaned over to Govinda and whispered into his ear: "Now I'll show the old man that I've learned something from him."

Taking up his stance right in front of the shramana and concentrating his mind, he captured the old man's gaze in his own, spellbound him, rendering him mute and will-less. He subjected him to his own will and commanded him silently to perform whatever was demanded of him. The old man was mute, his gaze fixed, his will disabled; his arms hung loose at his sides. He had been powerless to withstand Siddhartha's spell. The shramana fell under the control of Siddhartha's thoughts and he was forced to do whatever they commanded. So the old man bowed several times, made the gestures of giving his blessing, and haltingly uttered a pious formula wishing them well on their journey. The youths returned his bows with thanks, returned his good wishes, took their leave, and departed.

On the way, Govinda said: "Siddhartha, you learned more from the shramanas than I knew. It is difficult, very difficult, to bind an old shramana with a spell. Truly, if you had remained there, you would soon have learned to walk on water."

"I have no desire to walk on water," said Siddhartha. "Let old shramanas content themselves with such skills."

Gotama

IN THE CITY of Shravasti, every child knew the name of the exalted Buddha, and every household was ready to fill the alms bowls of the Buddha's silently begging disciples. Near the city lay Gotama's favorite dwelling place, the Jeta Grove, which had been presented to him and his followers as a gift by the wealthy merchant Anathapindika, an ardent devotee of the Exalted One.

The two young ascetics were led to this region by tales and the answers they received to their questions as they went along trying to learn Gotama's whereabouts. And when they arrived in Shravasti, food was offered to them at the very first house where they stopped to beg. They accepted the food, and Siddhartha asked the woman who gave it to them: "Generous lady, we would so much like to learn where the supremely Venerable One, the Buddha, is staying, for we are two shramanas from the forest and have come to see him, the Perfect One, and hear the teaching from his lips."

The woman replied: "You have truly come to the right place, you shramanas from the forest. Know that the Exalted One is staying in the Jeta Grove,

Anathapindika's garden. You can spend the night there, wayfarers, for there is enough room even for the countless seekers who flock to that place to hear the teaching from his lips."

Govinda was very happy and joyfully exclaimed: "Excellent! Our goal is reached and our journey is at an end! But tell us, mother of wayfarers, do you know the Buddha? Have you seen him with your own eyes?"

The woman replied: "I have seen the Exalted One many times. Many a day I have seen him passing through the streets, silent, in his yellow robe, holding out his alms bowl without speaking at the doors of the houses, and carrying his full bowl away."

Govinda listened rapt and was eager to ask the woman more questions. But Siddhartha urged him to move on. They said their thanks and continued their journey. They scarcely needed to ask the way, for there were quite a few mendicants and monks from Gotama's community on their way to the Jeta Grove. Since they reached the place at night, there were constant new arrivals, and incessant shouting and talking coming from those asking for a place to sleep and others allotting them one. The two shramanas, used to life in the forest, quickly and quietly found a place to lie down and rested there till morning.

By the dawn's light they saw with astonishment what a huge host of believers and curiosity seekers had spent the night there. Along all the paths of the magnificent grove, yellow-robed monks were moving. Here and there they sat beneath the trees absorbed in meditation or engaged in spiritual discourse. The shady gardens gave the impression of a city full of people, swarming like bees. The majority of monks were leaving with their alms bowls to gather food in the city for the midday meal, the only meal of the day. Even the Buddha himself, the Enlightened One, had the custom of going along on the morning begging round.

Siddhartha saw him and recognized him instantly, as though he had been pointed out by a god. He saw a plain man in a yellow habit, walking silently with his begging bowl in his hand.

"Look over there!" said Siddhartha softly to Govinda. "That one over there is the Buddha!"

All eyes, Govinda looked at the monk in the yellow habit, who seemed in no way distinct from the hundreds of other monks. But soon Govinda saw it too: It was him. And they followed him and watched.

The Buddha went his way humbly, absorbed in thought. His quiet face was neither happy nor sad; it gave the impression of a slight inward smile. The Buddha moved quietly, calmly, with a hidden smile, not unlike a healthy child. Just like all his monks he wore a robe and placed his feet precisely, according to precept. But his face and gait; his still, lowered gaze; his still, loose-hanging hand; and even every finger on his still, loose-hanging hand were expressions of peace, of perfection. Seeking nothing, emulating nothing, breathing gently, he moved in an atmosphere of imperishable calm, imperishable light, inviolable peace.

So Gotama went his way toward the city to gather

alms, and the two shramanas knew him only by the perfection of his calm, the stillness of his form, in which no seeking, wanting, imitating, or effort could be found, only light and peace.

"Today we shall hear the teaching from his lips," said Govinda.

Siddhartha did not reply. He was little interested in the teaching; he doubted it would contain anything new to him, since, like Govinda, he had repeatedly heard the content of this Buddhadharma, even if only second- or thirdhand. But he kept his eye attentively on the Buddha's head, his shoulders, his feet, on his still, loose hand; and it seemed to him that every joint on every finger of this hand was a teaching, that it spoke truth, breathed truth, smelled of truth, glowed with truth. This man, this Buddha, was in truth who he was even in the movements of his little fingers. This man was holy. Never had Siddhartha so venerated anyone, never had he loved a person as he loved this one.

The two youths followed the Buddha silently all the way into the city and back, since they planned to abstain from food that day themselves. They watched the Buddha return from the city and take his meal among his disciples. What he ate would not have satisfied a bird. Then they saw him withdraw into the shadows of the mango grove.

But in the evening, when the heat had subsided and everyone in the camp had revived and assembled, they heard the Buddha teach. They heard his voice, and that too was perfect, characterized by perfect calmness and

.peace. Gotama taught the teaching of suffering, the origin of suffering, and the path to the cessation of suffering. His quiet discourse flowed calm and clear. Life was suffering, the world was full of suffering, but liberation from suffering had been found. He who followed the path of the Buddha attained liberation.

With a gentle but firm voice, the Exalted One taught the four main truths and the eightfold path. Patiently he followed the customary course of the teaching, giving the examples and making the repetitions. His voice floated bright and still over the listeners like a light, like a sky full of stars.

When the Buddha ended his talk, night had already fallen. Many who had journeyed to see him came forward and asked to be accepted into the community, and took refuge in the teaching. And the Buddha accepted them by saying: "Well have you heard the teaching, and well has it been proclaimed. Enter into it then, and live in sacredness, so as to bring an end to suffering."

And behold, shy Govinda also stepped forward, and said: "I, too, take refuge in the Exalted One and his teaching," and requested to be accepted as a disciple. And he was accepted.

Immediately afterward, when the Buddha had withdrawn to take his night's rest, Govinda turned to Siddhartha and said animatedly: "Siddhartha, it is not my place to criticize you; but together we listened to the Exalted One, together we heard the teaching. Govinda heard the teaching, and he took refuge in it. But you, honorable friend, do you not wish to tread the path of liberation? Are you going to hesitate? Are you going to continue to wait?"

Siddhartha awoke as from sleep when he heard Govinda's words. He looked for a long time into Govinda's face. Then he spoke softly, in a voice without mockery: "Govinda, my friend, now you have taken the step, you have chosen your path. Always, Govinda, you have been my friend, and always you have been a step behind me. Often I thought: 'Is Govinda ever going to take a step on his own, without me, acting from his own heart?' And there it is: Now you have become a man and have chosen your own path. May you follow it to its end, my friend. May you attain liberation!"

Govinda, who did not yet fully understand, repeated his question in impatient tones: "Come on, now, my friend, out with it! Tell me that it could not be otherwise, but that you, my learned friend, will also take refuge in the exalted Buddha!"

Siddhartha laid his hand on Govinda's shoulder. "You did not listen to my words of aspiration for you and my blessing. I will repeat it. May you follow this path to the end. May you attain liberation!"

In this moment, Govinda realized his friend had left him, and he began to cry.

"Siddhartha!" he wailed.

Siddhartha spoke to him kindly. "Do not forget, Govinda, that you are now one of the Buddha's shramanas! You have given up home and parents, given up lineage and possessions, given up your own will, given up friendship. This is the requirement of the teaching, this is the requirement of the Exalted One. This is what you yourself wanted. Tomorrow, Govinda, I will leave you."

For a long time afterward, the two friends wandered in the trees; for a long time after they lay down, sleep did not come to them. Again and again, Govinda pressed his friend to tell him why he would not take refuge in the Buddha's teaching, what flaw he found in this teaching. But each time Siddhartha rebuffed him, saying: "Give it up, Govinda! The Exalted One's teaching is excellent; how should I find a flaw in it?"

At first light, a follower of the Buddha's, one of his oldest monks, went through the garden, calling everyone to him who had newly taken refuge in the teaching, so he could invest them with the yellow robe and instruct them in the initial precepts and duties of their new condition. Govinda pulled himself away from his childhood friend, embracing him one more time, and joined the procession of neophytes.

But Siddhartha wandered through the grove, thinking.

There Gotama, the Exalted One, encountered him. Siddhartha greeted him respectfully, and as the Buddha's gaze was so full of kindness and quietude, the youth took courage and asked the Venerable One's permission to address him. Without speaking, the Exalted One nodded his assent.

Siddhartha said: "Yesterday, O Exalted One, it was granted to me to hear your wondrous teaching. Together with my friend, I came from afar to hear the teaching. And now my friend is going to remain with you; he has taken refuge in you. I, however, am about to resume my wanderings."

"As you please," said the Venerable One politely.

"I speak far too boldly," Siddhartha continued, "but I would not like to leave the Exalted One without having straightforwardly communicated my thoughts to him. Would the Venerable One grant me a further moment's hearing?"

Silently the Buddha nodded assent.

Siddhartha said: "There is one thing in your teaching, most venerable sir, that I admire above everything else. Everything in your teaching is perfectly clear and irrefutable. You show the world as a never-broken, perfect chain, an eternal chain consisting of causes and their effects. Never has this been so clearly perceived and so incontrovertibly presented. Truly every brahmin's heart must beat faster in his breast when, through your teaching, he glimpses the world as a perfectly linked whole, without a break, clear as a crystal, not dependent on anything random, not dependent on the gods. Let us leave aside whether it is good or bad, whether life in it is suffering or joy—this may not be an essential question—but the unity of the world, the interdependence of everything that occurs, the inclusion of everything big and small within the same flow, the same law of causation, of becoming and passing away—this shines clearly forth from your exalted doctrine, O Perfect One. But now, according to your own doctrine, this unity and consistency of all things is nevertheless broken at one point; through one small gap, there flows into this world of unity something alien, new, something that did not exist before, that cannot be demonstrated and proven. This is your own teaching of the overcoming of the world, of liberation. But by this small gap, this small break, the unified and eternal cosmic lawfulness, is again quashed and invalidated. Please pardon me for bringing up this objection."

Gotama had listened to him quietly, unmoved. Now in his kindly, polite, and clear voice, the Perfect One spoke: "You have heard the teaching, brahmin's son. Good for you for having pondered it so deeply. You have found a gap in it, a flaw. May you continue to ponder that. But beware, you who are greedy for knowledge, of the jungle of opinions and the battle of words. Opinions are worth little. They can be beautiful or ugly, anyone can espouse or reject them. But the teaching that you heard from me is not my opinion, and its aim is not to explain the world to those who are greedy for knowledge. It has a different aim—liberation from suffering. This is what Gotama teaches, nothing else."

"Please do not be angry with me, Exalted One," the youth said. "It was not to contend with you, not to fight with you over words, that I spoke the way I did. You are indeed right; opinions are worth little. But allow me to say one thing more: Not for a moment have I doubted you. I have not doubted for a moment that you are a buddha, that you have attained the goal, the supreme goal, toward which so many thousands of brahmins and brahmin's sons strive. You have found liberation from death. This came to you as a result of your own seeking on your own path, through thought, through meditation, through realization, through enlightenment. It did not come to you through a teaching! And that is my idea, O Exalted One—nobody attains enlightenment through a teaching. O Venerable One, you will not be able to express to anyone through words and doctrine what happened to you in the moment of your enlightenment! Much is contained in the doctrine of the enlightened Buddha, much is taught in it—to live in an honest and upright way, to avoid evil. But there is one thing that this so clear and so venerable teaching does not contain; it does not contain the mystery of what the Exalted One himself experienced, he alone among hundreds of thousands. This is what I understood and realized when I listened to the teaching. This is the reason I am going to continue my wandering—not to find another or a better teaching, for I know that one does not exist, but in order to leave behind all teachings and all teachers and to attain my goal on my own or die. But many a time will I recall this day, O Exalted One, and this moment when my eyes have beheld a holy man."

The Buddha gazed at the ground in stillness; his inscrutable countenance remained still in perfect equanimity.

"May your thoughts," the Venerable One said slowly, "not be false ones. May you reach the goal! But tell me: Have you seen the host of my shramanas, my many brothers who have taken refuge in the teaching? And do you believe, unknown shramana, that it would be better for all of them to abandon the teaching and return to the life of the world and its pleasures?"

"Such an idea is far from my mind," exclaimed Siddhartha. "May they all remain with the teaching, may they all reach their goal! It is not for me to judge the life of another! It is only for myself that I must judge, that I must choose and refuse. Liberation from ego is what we shramanas are seeking, O Exalted One. If I were your disciple, O Venerable One, I am afraid it might befall me that my ego would be pacified and liberated only seemingly, only illusorily, that in reality it would survive and grow great, for then I would make the teaching, my discipleship, my love of you, and the community of monks into my ego!"

With a half smile, with an unshakable brightness and kindliness, Gotama looked the stranger in the eye and dismissed him with a scarcely visible gesture.

"You are clever, shramana," said the Venerable One. "You know how to speak cleverly, my friend. Beware of excessive cleverness!"

The Buddha moved on, and his gaze and his half smile remained engraved in Siddhartha's memory forever.

I have never seen anyone with such a gaze, I have never seen anyone smile, sit, and walk in such a way, he thought. In truth that is just the way I would like to be able to gaze, smile, sit, and walk—so free, so worthy, so hidden, so open, so childlike, and so mysterious. Truly only a person who has penetrated to the inmost part of his self gazes and walks like that. I, too, shall surely try to penetrate to the inmost part of my self.

I have seen a man, one and only one, Siddhartha thought, before whom I had to lower my gaze. Before no other will I ever lower my gaze, no other. No other teaching will seduce me, since this teaching has not seduced me.

The Buddha robbed me, thought Siddhartha, he robbed me, yet he gave me even more. He robbed me of my friend, who believed in me and now believes in him, who was my shadow and is now Gotama's shadow. But he gave me Siddhartha, he gave me myself.

Awakening

As Siddhartha left the grove, leaving the Buddha, the Perfect One, behind, leaving Govinda behind, he had the feeling he was also leaving behind in the grove his life up to that time and separating himself from it. He pondered this feeling, which completely filled him, as he slowly made his way. He pondered deeply, sinking down into the depths of this feeling as through deep water, until he reached the point where the causes lie—for to know the causes, so it seemed to him, that is what thinking is, and only in this way do feelings become knowledge instead of being wasted; in this way they become meaningful and begin to radiate what is within them.

Going slowly along his way, Siddhartha deliberated. He realized that he was no longer a youth but had become a man. He realized that there was one thing he had left behind as a snake leaves behind an old skin, one thing that was no longer in him that had accompanied him throughout his youth and been a part of him—the desire to have a teacher and to hear teachings. The last teacher he had encountered on his way, he had left, even him, the highest and wisest teacher, the most holy one, the Buddha. He had had to part from him; he had been unable to accept his teaching.

Slower yet the pondering man walked, asking himself: "But now what is it that you were trying to learn from teachers and teachings, and what is it that they, though they taught you a lot, could not teach you?" And he found this: It was the ego whose meaning and essence I wanted to learn. It was the ego that I wanted to get rid of, to overcome. But I was unable to overcome it, I could only trick it, could only elude it, could only hide from it. In truth nothing in the world has occupied my thoughts so much as my ego, this enigma that I am alive, that I am unique and separate and distinct from all others, that I am Siddhartha! And there is nothing in the world I know less about than me, than Siddhartha!

The slowly walking thinker came to a halt altogether, captured by this last thought, and immediately from this thought another sprang, a new thought, which was this: That I know nothing of myself, that Siddhartha remains so alien and unknown to me—there is one cause for this, just one: I was afraid of myself, I was running away from myself! I was looking for atman, I was looking for Brahman; I was determined to tear my ego apart, to peel it layer by layer in order to find in its unknown innards the pith behind all the husks, atman, life, the divine, the ultimate. But in the process I myself got lost.

Siddhartha opened his eyes and looked around him. A smile spread over his face, and a profound sensation of awakening from a long dream filled him down to his toes. Immediately he resumed walking, walking fast, like a man who knows what it is he has to do.

Oh, he thought, taking deep breaths, now I will not let Siddhartha slip away from me again! No more will the point of departure for my thinking and my life be atman and the suffering of the world. I will no longer kill myself and tear myself to pieces, trying to find the secret beneath the rubble. The *Yogaveda* will teach me no longer, nor the *Atharvaveda*, nor the ascetics, nor any other teaching. I will learn from myself, be my own student. I will learn about myself, about the mystery of Siddhartha.

He looked around him as though he were seeing the world for the first time. The world was beautiful, full of colors, strange and enigmatic. Here was blue, here yellow, here green, the sky was in movement and so was the river; the forest was fixed in place and so were the hills—all beautiful, all mysterious and magical. And in the middle of it all was Siddhartha, the awakened one, on the path to himself. All of it, all the yellow and blue, the river and the forest, entered Siddhartha for the first time through his eyes. It was no longer the magical deception of Mara, was no longer the veil of Maya, was no longer the meaningless and arbitrary multiplicity of the world of appearances contemptuously derided by deep-thinking brahmins, who scorned multiplicity and sought unity. Blue was blue, river was river, and even if in the blue and the river the divine and the one were alive in Siddhartha in a hidden way, it was still the divine way and intention to be yellow here, blue here, sky here, forest here, and Siddhartha here. Meaning and essence were not somewhere behind things, they were in them, in them all.

How deaf and dumb I have been! thought the traveler moving quickly along his way. When one is reading a text whose meaning he is seeking, he does not scorn the signs and letters as deceptions, accidents, and worthless husks; rather he reads them, he studies them, he loves them, letter by letter. But I was trying to read the book of the world and the book of my own being, and because of my preconceptions I scorned the signs and letters, I called them the deception of the world of appearances, I called my eyes and my tongue arbitrary and worthless phenomena. No, it is over now! I have awakened, I have really awakened, and have only today been born!

As Siddhartha was thinking these thoughts, he came to a halt again, suddenly, as though a snake lay on the path. For suddenly this too became clear to him: Since he was really and truly like someone freshly awakened or like a newborn, he had to begin his life all over again from the beginning. When he had left the Jeta Grove, the grove of the Exalted One, in the morning, already awakened, already on the way to himself, it had been his intention—one that seemed natural and self-evident—to return after his years of asceticism to his home and his father. But now, just in this moment in which he came to a halt as though a snake lay on his path, he awoke also to this insight: I am really no longer who I was before. I am no longer an ascetic, no longer a priest, no longer a brahmin. So what could I do at home with my father? Study? Perform sacrificial rites? Practice meditation? All this is over and done with; this is not what lies ahead of me anymore.

Siddhartha continued to stand there motionless, and for the period of a heartbeat and a breath his heart went cold; he felt it go cold in his breast like a small animal— a bird or a rabbit—when he realized how alone he was. For years he had been homeless and not felt it. Now he felt it. Up till now, even in his deepest meditative absorption, he had been his father's son, a brahmin of high standing, a spiritual person. Now he was only Siddhartha, the awakened one, and nothing else. He drew in a deep breath, and for a moment he was cold and shivered. No one was as alone as he was—no nobleman separated from other noblemen or artisan separated from other artisans, no longer having the shelter of their company, no longer sharing their life and their talk. No brahmin who was no longer accounted a brahmin and no longer lived with brahmins, no ascetic who had found refuge in his status as a shramana—even the most forlorn hermit in the forest was not as singular and alone, for even the hermit was wrapped in his association with something, even he was part of a group that harbored him. Govinda had become a monk, and a thousand monks were his brothers, wore the same garment, believed his beliefs, spoke as he did. But he, Siddhartha, what was he part of? Whose life could he share? Whose speech could he speak?

Out of this moment, in which the world melted away from around him, in which he was alone like a star in the sky—out of this moment of frigidity and dejection, Siddhartha arose more of an ego than ever before, more tightly clenched within. His feeling was: That was the last shudder of awakening, the last pang of birth. And immediately he resumed his journey, walking with haste and impatience, no longer back in the direction of home or father, not back anywhere.

PART TWO

Kamala

SIDDHARTHA LEARNED something new every step of the way. For the world had been transformed, and his heart was enraptured. He saw the sun rise over the wooded hills and go down over the distant palm-lined shore. At night he saw the stars arrayed across the sky and the crescent moon floating like a boat in the blue. He saw trees, stars, animals, clouds, rainbows, rocks, herbs, flowers, streams and rivers, dew glittering on the brush in the morning, distant lofty peaks blue and pale; birds and bees sang their songs, the wind blew silver in the rice fields. These myriads of colorful things had always been there; the sun and moon had always shone, rivers had always rushed and bees hummed. But in former days all this had been nothing more for Siddhartha than a transitory and beguiling veil before his eyes, viewed with distrust, meant to be punctured by thought and destroyed, since it was not the essence, since the essence lay beyond the visible. But now his un-fettered vision dwelt here—he saw and acknowledged the visible, sought his home in this world. He no longer pursued the essence or looked toward the beyond. The world was beautiful when one just looked at it without looking for anything, just simply, as a child. The moon and stars were beautiful, brook and bank, forest and rock, goat and beetle, flower and butterfly—all were beautiful. It was sweet and beautiful to walk through the world in this way, so like a child, so awake, so open to whatever lay at hand, so without suspicion. The sun blazed down on his head in a different way, the forest shadows cooled him differently, water from the streams and cisterns tasted different, as did the squashes and bananas. The days were short, the nights were short, each hour flowed swiftly by, like a sail on the sea—and under that sail a ship full of treasure, full of joys. Siddhartha saw a tribe of apes moving through the forest vaults, in the high branches, and heard a wild litany of lust. Siddhartha saw a ram pursue a ewe and mate with her. Siddhartha saw a pike hunting in a reedy lake in its evening hunger, and the fearful young fish propelling themselves out of the water, fluttering and flashing, in swarms before him. And force and passion rose urgently out of the rushing whirlpools the impetuous hunter created.

All of this had always been there, and he had not seen it. He had not been there with it. Now he was there with it, and was part of it. Light and shadow passed through his eyes, the stars and moon through his heart.

As he traveled, Siddhartha also recalled everything he had experienced in the Jeta Grove, the teaching he had heard there, the divine Buddha, his parting from Govinda, his conversation with the Exalted One. He

remembered again the words he had spoken to the Exalted One, every word, and with astonishment he realized that he had said things then that he actually did
not know at all yet. What he had said to Gotama: that
his, the Buddha's, treasure and secret was not the teaching but rather the ineffable and unteachable thing that
he had experienced at the moment of his enlightenment—it was this, this very thing, that he was now setting forth to experience, that he was now beginning to
experience. Himself was what he now had to experience. Of course he had known for a long time that his
self was atman, of the same eternal essence as Brahman.
But he had never really found this self, because he had
been trying to catch it in the net of thought. It was a
certainty that the body was not the self, nor was the play
of the senses; but it was also not thinking, not the
reasoning mind, not wisdom that could be learned,
and not the learnable art of deduction and spinning
new ideas out of old ones. No, the realm of ideas
also was part of this world, and nothing worthwhile
was achieved through destroying the unreal ego of
the senses at the expense of bloating up the unreal ego
of ideas and erudition. Both of them—ideas and the
senses—were fine things, behind both of them the ultimate meaning lay hidden, both were worth heeding, it
was worth playing with both of them, neither despising
nor overrating them. The secret voice of the inmost
essence could be overheard in both of them. He wished
to strive for nothing but what the voice commanded
him to strive for, stay nowhere but where the voice

counseled. Why did Gotama once, in the hour of hours, sit down beneath the Bodhi Tree, where enlightenment came upon him? He had heard a voice, a voice in his own heart, which commanded him to seek rest under this tree, and he had not opted instead for austerities, sacrifices, baths, or prayer, not for eating or drinking, not for sleep or dream—he had obeyed the voice. Obeying in this way—not an outer command, but only the voice—to be ready to do that was good, was necessary; nothing else was necessary.

One night, sleeping in the straw hut of a ferryman by a river, Siddhartha had a dream. Govinda stood before him in a yellow ascetic's robe. Govinda looked sad, and sadly he asked, "Why have you abandoned me?" Then he embraced Govinda, threw his arms around him, and as he held him to his breast and kissed him, it was no longer Govinda but a woman, and a full breast popped out of the woman's garment, on which Siddhartha rested his head and drank. The milk from this breast tasted sweet and strong. It tasted of woman and man, of sun and forest, of beast and flower, of every fruit, of every desire. It made one drunk and unaware.

When Siddhartha awoke, the pale river glimmered through the door of the hut, and in the forest, deep and melodious, sounded the dark hooting of an owl.

With the coming of day, Siddhartha asked his host the ferryman to take him to the other side of the river. The ferryman took him across the river on his bamboo raft. The sun shone ruddy on the broad waters in the morning light.

"That's a beautiful river," Siddhartha said to his companion.

"Yes," said the ferryman, "a very beautiful river. I love it more than anything. I have often listened to it speak, often looked it in the eye, and I have always learned from it. One can learn a lot from a river."

"I thank you, benefactor," said Siddhartha, as he climbed onto the far bank. "I have no gift for your hospitality, my friend, and nothing to pay your fee. I am a homeless one, a brahmin's son and a shramana."

"I saw that clearly enough," said the ferryman, "and I wasn't expecting any fee from you, nor a gift for my hospitality either. You can give me the gift another time."

"You think so?" said Siddhartha, amused.

"For sure. I have learned that from the river too—everything comes back again. You, too, shramana, will come back. Now, farewell! Let your friendship be my fee. Keep me in mind when you make sacrifices to the gods."

Smiling, they said their good-byes. Siddhartha smiled with happiness over the ferryman's friendship and kindness. He is like Govinda, he thought as he smiled. Everyone I meet on my way is like Govinda. They are all grateful, although they themselves are due the gratitude. All of them treat me with deference; they would all be happy to be my friend, they would be glad to obey me without having to think too much. People are children.

Around noon he came to a village. In the lane in

front of the mud huts children were rolling about on the ground, playing with seeds and shells, screaming and scuffling; but they all fled shyly before the strange shramana. At the far end of the village, the way led over a stream, and on the stream's brink a young woman was kneeling and washing clothes. Siddhartha greeted her, and she raised her head and looked up at him and smiled so that he could see the whites of her eyes gleaming. He called out a blessing to her in the manner of travelers, and asked her how far he still had to go to the big city. She stood up and approached him. Her moist mouth glistened in her young face. She bantered with him a little and asked him if he had already eaten and if it was true that at night shramanas slept by themselves in the forest and were not allowed to have women. At the same time, she put her left foot on top of his right and made the movement women make when they are enticing a man to make love to them in the style known in the textbooks as "climbing a tree." Siddhartha felt his blood heating up, and because his dream returned to his mind at that moment, he bent down over the woman and kissed the brown tip of her breast with his lips. Looking up, he saw her smiling face, filled with desire, and her narrowed eyes pleading with longing.

Siddhartha also felt longing and felt his sexuality stir, but since he had never yet touched a woman, he hesitated a moment, just as his hands were reaching out to take hold of her. And in this moment, with a shudder he heard his inner voice, and the voice said no. All the magic vanished from the smiling face of the young woman. All he now saw was the moist gaze of a rutting female animal. Kindly he stroked her cheek, turned away from her, and melted nimbly away into the bamboo thicket before her disappointed eyes.

On that day, before evening, he reached a big city, and was glad, for he was longing for human company. He had long been living in the forest, and the ferryman's straw hut, in which he had slept the previous night, was the first roof he had had over his head for a long time.

On the edge of the city, by a beautiful cloistered grove, the wanderer came upon a small procession of male and female servants laden with baskets. In their midst, in an ornate litter carried by four servants, sat a woman, their mistress, on red cushions under a multicolored canopy. Siddhartha remained standing at the entrance to the pleasure grove and watched the procession. His eye fell upon the male servants and the female servants, upon the litter, and upon the lady in the litter. Beneath black hair coifed high on her head, he saw a very bright, very tender, very intelligent face, a bright red mouth like a fig newly broken open, eyebrows that had been trained and painted into lofty arches, dark eyes, intelligent and alert, a pale long neck emerging from a green and gold mantle, and pale hands resting loose, long and narrow, with broad gold bands at the wrists.

Siddhartha saw how beautiful she was, and his heart laughed. He bowed low as the litter passed by him, and when he straightened up again, looked into that bright gracious face, read for a moment what was written in the clever eyes beneath their lofty arches, and drew in a whiff of an unfamiliar fragrance. Smiling, the beautiful woman briefly nodded to him, then vanished into the grove, followed by her servants.

This is the way I enter this city, thought Siddhartha— under a gracious sign. He felt drawn to enter the grove immediately, but he reconsidered and for the first time became aware of how the servants and maids at the entrance had looked at him, how disdainfully, with what suspicion, what rejection.

I am still a shramana, he thought, still an ascetic and a beggar. I cannot stay like that; like that I cannot enter the grove. And he laughed.

The next person who came along the road he asked about the grove and the name of the woman. He learned that it was the grove belonging to Kamala, the famous courtesan, and that in addition to the grove, she owned a house in the city.

Then he entered the city. He had an aim now.

Following this aim, he let himself be swallowed up by the city. He moved with the flow in the streets, stood still in the plazas, rested on the stone steps by the river. Toward evening he made friends with a barber's assistant whom he had seen working in the shadow of an archway and met again praying in a temple of Vishnu. He told him stories about Vishnu and Lakshmi. He slept the night by the boats on the river, and early in the morning, before the first customers arrived in the shop, he had the barber's assistant shave off his beard and cut and comb his hair and anoint it with fine oil. Then he bathed in the river.

When the beautiful Kamala approached her grove in the litter in the late afternoon, Siddhartha was there at the entrance. He bowed and received the courtesan's greeting. Then he beckoned to the servant who came last in her train and asked him to tell his mistress that a young brahmin desired to speak with her. After a while the servant came back, asked the waiting youth to follow him, led him in silence into a pavilion where Kamala lay on a couch, and left him alone with her.

"Were you not standing outside there yesterday, and did you not greet me?"

"Yes, I did see you yesterday and I greeted you."

"But yesterday were you not wearing a beard, and did you not have long hair with dust in it?"

"You observed keenly and saw everything. You saw Siddhartha the brahmin's son, who left his home to become a shramana and who was a shramana for three years. Now, however, having abandoned that path, I have come to this city. And the first person I encountered before entering the city was you. I have come to you, O Kamala, to say this: You are the first woman to whom Siddhartha has spoken other than with downcast eyes. Never again shall I lower my eyes when I encounter a beautiful woman."

Kamala smiled and toyed with her fan of peacock feathers. And asked: "Was it only to tell me this that Siddhartha came to me?"

"To tell you this and to thank you for being so beautiful. And if it does not displease you, I would like to ask you, Kamala, to be my friend and my teacher, for as yet I know nothing of the art of which you are a master."

At this Kamala laughed out loud.

"Never before has it happened to me that a shramana came to me out of the forest and wanted to become my student! Never has it happened to me that a shramana with long hair and in an old tattered loincloth came to me. Many youths come to me, and brahmins' sons are among them, but they come in beautiful clothes, they come in fine shoes, they have perfume in their hair and money in their purses. That is the quality of the youths, shramana, who come to me."

Siddhartha said: "I am already beginning to learn from you. Yesterday, too, I learned something. I have gotten rid of the beard and had my hair combed and oiled. I only still lack a little bit, excellent lady: fine clothes, fine shoes, and money in my purse. Know that Siddhartha has undertaken more difficult things than these trifles and achieved them. How shall I not achieve what I set myself as a goal yesterday: to be your friend and to learn the joys of love from you! You shall see how fast I learn, Kamala. I have learned harder things than what you shall teach me. And so now: Is Siddhartha not good enough for you as he is—with oil in his hair, but without clothes, without shoes, without money?"

Laughing, Kamala exclaimed: "No, estimable friend, he is not good enough yet. He must have clothes, beautiful clothes, handsome shoes, plenty of money in his purse—and gifts for Kamala. Do you understand now, shramana from the forest? Are you taking this in?"

"I definitely am taking it in," Siddhartha exclaimed. "How could I fail to take in what comes out of such a mouth! Your mouth is like a fig freshly broken open, Kamala. And my mouth, too, is red and fresh, a fitting match for yours, you will see. But tell me, beautiful Kamala, have you no fear whatever of the shramana from the forest who has come to you to learn love?"

"Why should I be afraid of a shramana, a stupid shramana from the forest, who comes from among the jackals and has no idea what a woman is?"

"Oh, he's a strong one, the shramana, and is afraid of nothing. He might use force on you, beautiful maid. He might carry you off. He might hurt you."

"No, shramana, I have no fear of that. Has a shramana or a brahmin ever been afraid that someone might come and get him and steal his erudition, his piety, and his profundity? No, because they are really part of him, and he gives of them only what he wishes and to whom he wishes. That is the way it is, and it is just the same with Kamala and the joys of love. Kamala's mouth is beautiful and red, but try to kiss it against Kamala's will and you will get not a drop of sweetness from it, though it is capable of imparting so much sweetness! You are a fast learner, Siddhartha, so learn this too: You can beg love, buy it, receive it as a gift, or find it on the street, but you cannot steal it. That is a misguided approach you have come up with there. No, it would be a shame for such a handsome young fellow to grab the wrong end of the stick like that."

Siddhartha bowed with a smile. "It would be a shame, Kamala, how right you are! It would be a terrible shame. No, I shall not lose one drop of your mouth's sweetness, nor you of mine! So let us leave it at this: Siddhartha will return when he has what he is now lacking: clothes, shoes, and money. But say, gracious Kamala, can you not spare me a little advice?"

"Advice? Why not? Who would not want to give a poor, ignorant shramana who comes from the jackals in the forest a piece of advice?"

"So then, dear Kamala, advise me: Where should I go to find those three things the fastest?"

"Friend, that is a thing many people would like to know. You must do what you have learned to do, and get money and clothes and shoes for it. There is no other way for a poor man to get money. What can you do?"

"I can think, I can wait, and I can fast."

"Is that all?"

"That is all. No, I can also compose poetry. Will you give me a kiss for a poem?"

"Yes, I will, if I like the poem. How does it go?"

After thinking for a moment, Siddhartha recited the following verse:

Into her shady grove passed the beautiful Kamala,
At the entrance to the grove stood the sun-
    browned shramana.

Seeing this lotus blossom, he bowed low.
Kamala repaid him with a smile,
And the youth thought: Sweeter than offering to
    the gods
Is offering to the beautiful Kamala.

Kamala clapped so hard that her golden bracelets jangled.

"Your verses are beautiful, sun-browned shramana, and truly I will not come out behind if I give you a kiss for them."

She drew him to her with her eyes, he lowered his face to hers, and he laid his mouth on that mouth that was like a fig freshly broken open. Kamala kissed him for a long time, and with profound astonishment Siddhartha felt her teaching him, felt her wisdom, felt her control—rebuffing him, luring him on—and he felt that behind this first long kiss, a long well-ordered, well-proven series of kisses awaited him, each different from the others. Breathing deeply, he remained standing there, and at this moment he was like a child bewildered by the abundance of knowledge and things worthy of learning that had been revealed to him.

"Your verses are very beautiful," exclaimed Kamala. "If I were rich, I would give you pieces of gold for them. But it will be hard for you to acquire as much money as you need with poetry. For you need a great deal of money if you want to be Kamala's friend."

"How you can kiss!" Siddhartha blurted out.

"Yes, so I can. That is why I have no lack of clothes,

shoes, bracelets, and all manner of beautiful things. But what is to become of you? Is there nothing you can do besides thinking, fasting, and composing poetry?"

"I also know the sacrificial liturgy," Siddhartha said, "but I do not want to chant it anymore. I also know magic incantations, but I no longer wish to pronounce them. I have read the scriptures—"

"Enough!" Kamala interrupted him. "You can read and write?"

"I can certainly do that. A lot of people can."

"Most people cannot. I cannot do so myself. It is very good that you can read and write, very good. And the magic incantations—you will be able to use those too."

At this moment a servant woman came running in and whispered a message in her mistress's ear.

"I have a visitor coming," said Kamala. "Be gone at once, Siddhartha. No one must see you here, do you understand? I shall see you again tomorrow."

She ordered the maid to give the pious brahmin a white outer robe. Before he knew what was happening to him, Siddhartha found himself being pulled away by the maid and led by a circuitous route to a shed in the garden. He was given a robe, led into the bushes, and emphatically warned to vanish immediately and unseen from the grove.

He gladly did what he was told. As accustomed to the forest as he was, he had no trouble getting noiselessly out of the grove and over the hedge. Happily he went back into the city, carrying the rolled-up robe under his arm. He stationed himself at the entrance to an inn used by travelers, begged silently for some food, and silently accepted a piece of rice cake. Maybe by tomorrow, he thought, I shall no longer be asking people for food.

Pride flared up suddenly within him. He was no longer a shramana; it was no longer fitting for him to beg. He gave the rice cake to a dog and did without eating.

This worldly life is easy, thought Siddhartha. There is nothing difficult in it. Everything was hard, and in the end, hopeless, when I was a shramana. Now everything is easy, easy like the kissing lesson that Kamala gave me. I need clothes and money, and that is all. Those are trivial, easily fulfilled goals, nothing worth losing sleep over.

He had long since learned the location of Kamala's house in the city. The following day he appeared there.

"Things are going well," she told him. "You are expected at Kamaswami's house. He is the city's richest merchant. If he likes you, he will take you into his service. Be smart, sun-browned shramana. I have had other people tell him about you. Show him your good side— he is very powerful. But do not be too humble! I do not want you becoming his servant. You have to become his equal, otherwise I will not be happy with you. Kamaswami is starting to get old and complacent. If he likes you, he will entrust a lot of his business to you."

Siddhartha thanked her and laughed. When she found out that he had had nothing to eat that day or the day before, she had bread and fruit brought, and she served him herself.

"You have been lucky," she said in parting. "One door after the other is opening for you. Why is that happening? Have you worked some magic?"

Siddhartha said: "Yesterday I told you I knew how to think, to wait, and to fast, and you thought these worthless skills. But they are worth a lot, Kamala, you will see. You will see that the stupid shramanas from the forest learn a great deal and can do a lot of excellent things that you all cannot do. The day before yesterday I was still an unkempt beggar, by yesterday I had already kissed Kamala, and soon I will be a merchant and have money and all those things that you think valuable."

"Well, yes," she admitted, "but where would you be without me? How would things be with you without Kamala's help?"

"Dear Kamala," said Siddhartha, pulling himself up to his full height, "when I came to see you in your grove, I was taking the first step. It was my intention to learn love from this most beautiful of women. From the very moment that I formed this intention, I also knew that I would carry it out. I knew that you would help me—with the first look you gave me at the entrance to the grove, I knew it already."

"And if I had not been willing?"

"You were willing. See here, Kamala: When you throw a stone into water, it falls quickly by the fastest route to the bottom of the pond. This is the way it is when Siddhartha has an aim, an intention. Siddhartha does nothing—he waits, he thinks, he fasts—but he passes through the things of the world like the stone through the water, without bestirring himself. He is drawn forward and he lets himself fall. His goal draws him to it, for he lets nothing enter his mind that interferes with the goal. This is what Siddhartha learned from the shramanas. This is what fools call magic, thinking that it is brought about by demons. Nothing is brought about by demons; demons do not exist. Anyone can do magic, anyone can reach his goals if he can think, wait, and fast."

Kamala heard him out. She loved his voice, she loved his gaze.

"Maybe it is as you say," she said softly. "But maybe it is also the case that Siddhartha is a good looking man, that women like the way he looks at them, and that is the reason good fortune comes his way."

With a kiss, Siddhartha took his leave. "May it be as you say, teacher. May my eyes' glance ever please you. May good fortune ever come to me from you."

Among the Child People

SIDDHARTHA WENT to see the merchant Kamaswami. He was shown into an opulent house. Servants led him over costly carpets into a chamber where the master of the house was waiting.

Kamaswami entered, a brisk, sleek man with thick graying hair; very intelligent, cautious eyes; and a sensual mouth. Master and guest greeted each other warmly.

"I have been told," said the merchant, "that you are a brahmin, a learned man, but that you are seeking service with a merchant. Have you fallen on hard times, brahmin, that you are looking for such work?"

"No," said Siddhartha, "I have not fallen on hard times, nor have I ever known hard times. Know that I come from the shramanas, with whom I lived for a long time."

"If you come from the shramanas, how could you not be hard up? Are not the shramanas completely without possessions?"

"I am indeed without possessions," said Siddhartha, "if that is what you mean. It is a fact that I am without possessions. But I am that way of my own free will and am therefore not hard up."

"But what do you expect to live from if you have no possessions?"

"I have never thought about it, my lord. I have been without possessions for more than three years and have never thought about what I should live from."

"So you lived off the wealth of others."

"I suppose that is the case. But a merchant also lives from what others have."

"Well said. He takes from others what is theirs, but not for nothing. He gives them wares in exchange."

"That indeed seems to be the way things are. Everyone takes, everyone gives—such is life."

"But permit me: If you are without possessions, what can you expect to give?"

"Everyone gives what he has. The warrior gives strength, the merchant gives merchandise, the teacher teaching, the farmer rice, the fisherman fish."

"Fine, fine. And so what is it now that you have to give? What have you learned, what can you do?"

"I can think, I can wait, I can fast."

"Is that all?"

"I think that is all."

"And what is that good for? For example, fasting, what is it good for?"

"It is an excellent thing, my lord. When a person has nothing to eat, then fasting is the most intelligent thing he can do. If, for example, Siddhartha had not learned to fast, then today he would have to take on just any work at all, if not with you, then anywhere, because hunger would force him to it. But Siddhartha can calmly wait, he knows no impatience, no state of need; he can withstand a siege of hunger for a long time and laugh too. That, my lord, is what fasting is good for."

"You are right, shramana. Wait a minute."

Kamaswami left and came back with a scroll, which he handed to his guest and asked: "Can you read this?"

Siddhartha looked at the scroll, on which a sales contract was written, and began to read out its contents.

"Superb," said Kamaswami. "And would you write something for me on this sheet?"

He gave him a piece of paper and a pen. Siddhartha wrote and gave the sheet back.

Kamaswami read: "Writing is good, thinking is better. Cleverness is good, patience is better."

"You are a first-rate writer," the merchant praised. "We have many things still to talk about. For today, I invite you to be my guest and reside in my house."

Siddhartha thanked him and accepted. He now lived in the house of the merchant. Clothes were brought to him and shoes, and a servant drew a bath for him every day. Twice a day an opulent meal was brought up to him, but Siddhartha ate only once a day, and neither ate meat nor drank wine. Kamaswami told him about his business, showed him his merchandise and his warehouse, showed him his accounts. Siddhartha became acquainted with many new things. He listened a great deal and spoke little. And remembering Kamala's words, he never subordinated himself to the merchant, forcing him to treat him as his equal or more than his equal. Kamaswami ran his business with painstaking care and often with passion, but Siddhartha regarded all this as a game whose rules he made every effort to learn but whose content never touched his heart.

He was not in Kamaswami's house long before he began to take part in his landlord's business. But every day, at the time she told him, he visited the beautiful Kamala, wearing handsome clothes and fine shoes, and soon he was bringing her gifts too. He learned much from her red, intelligent mouth. He learned much from her soft, supple hand. He was still a mere boy in matters of love and tended to throw himself blindly and insatiably into his pleasures as though into a bottomless pit, but she introduced him from the beginning to the doctrine that one cannot take pleasure without giving it, and that each gesture, each caress, each touch, each glance, each smallest part of the body has its own secret, which brings happiness to the one who knows how to draw it into the open. She taught him that lovers should never part after their feast of love without expressing admiration to one another, without owning oneself as much the conquered as the conqueror, so that neither party experiences satiety or emptiness nor the nasty feeling of having merely used the other or been merely used. Wondrous hours he spent in the company of the beautiful and intelligent virtuoso. He became her student, her lover, and her friend. Here with Kamala lay at this time the value and meaning of his life, not in Kamaswami's business.

The merchant taught him how to write important letters and contracts and became accustomed to consulting him on all matters of importance. He was quick to see that Siddhartha understood little about rice and wool, ships' voyages and business dealings, but that he had a lucky touch, and that Siddhartha exceeded his own ability for calmness and equanimity, in the art of listening, and in seeing into the hearts of strangers. "This brahmin," he said to a friend of his, "is no real merchant and will never be one, nor does he have a passion for business. But he possesses the secret of one to whom success comes by itself, whether because he was born under the right star, whether as a result of magic, or on account of something he learned from the shramanas. He always gives the impression of merely toying with business dealings. He never gets truly involved in them, they never dominate his mind; he never fears failure, is never bothered by loss."

The merchant's friend gave him this advice: "Give him a third of the profit of the business he does for you, but let him also bear the same percentage of the loss if a loss occurs. That will arouse some enthusiasm."

Kamaswami followed this advice. Siddhartha, however, paid little attention. If he made a profit, he took it in without emotion. If he made a loss, he laughed and said, "Oh, my, this did not go well."

It really seemed as though he was indifferent to business. Once he traveled to a village to buy up a large rice crop. But when he arrived the rice had already been sold to another dealer. Nevertheless, Siddhartha remained a number of days in that village, hosted the farmers, gave their children copper coins, joined in a wedding celebration, and came back from the journey quite content. Kamaswami took him to task for not coming back immediately, for wasting time and money. Siddhartha responded: "Give up your scolding, my friend! Nothing has ever been achieved by scolding. If we have taken a loss, then let me stand the loss. I am very content with this trip. I got to know a lot of people, I made friends with a brahmin, I had children sitting on my lap, farmers showed me their fields, no one treated me like a merchant."

"That's all quite lovely," exclaimed Kamaswami indignantly, "but you are in fact a merchant, or so I thought. Or was that just a pleasure trip you took?"

"Definitely," laughed Siddhartha, "I definitely took that trip for pleasure. Why else? I got to know people and places, I enjoyed hospitality and trust, I found friendship. You see, my friend, if I had been Kamaswami, as soon as I saw that my business deal was foiled, I would have turned around instantly and come back home totally upset. The time and money would in fact have been lost. But in my case I had a good few days, learned things, had a good time, and harmed neither myself nor anyone else through anger or haste. And if I ever go back there, perhaps to buy a future crop—or for whatever purpose—I will be warmly and kindly received by friendly people, and I will congratulate myself for not having been abrupt or shown irritation the last time. So let well enough alone, my friend, and do not harm yourself by scolding me. If the day comes when you see that Siddhartha is doing you damage, just say the word and Siddhartha will be on his way. But until that time, let us be content with one another."

The merchant's attempts to convince Siddhartha that he was eating his, Kamaswami's, bread were also in vain. Siddhartha was eating his own bread, or rather they were both eating other people's bread, everyone's bread. Never did Siddhartha have an ear for Kamaswami's worries, and Kamaswami worried a lot. If a business deal was in progress that threatened to fail, if his goods shipment seemed to be lost, if a debtor seemed unable to pay, never could Kamaswami convince his colleague that it was useful to waste words on worry or anger, to furrow one's brow, to sleep badly. Once when Kamaswami was reproaching him by saying he had learned everything he knew from him, Siddhartha replied as follows: "You will have to come up with better jokes than that! From you I have learned how much a basket of fish costs and how much interest you can demand on borrowed money. But that is not real knowledge. I did not learn thinking from you, dear Kamaswami—better you should try to learn it from me."

In truth his heart was not in the business. His business deals had the virtue of producing money for Kamala, and they produced a lot more than he needed for that. Aside from that, Siddhartha's only interest and curiosity was for the people whose business dealings, handwork, cares, pleasures, and follies had formerly been as alien and remote to him as the moon. As easy as it was for him to talk to everyone, get along with everyone, learn from everyone, to that very extent there was something that separated him from these people, this was clear to him. And this thing that set him apart was his being a shramana. He saw people going through their lives in the manner of a child or an animal, and he both loved and disdained this at the same time. He saw them striving—and suffering and getting gray—over things that seemed to him completely unworthy of this price: over money, over small pleasures, over a little respect. He saw them chiding and insulting one another, he saw them bemoaning pains that the shramanas smiled over and suffering from privations that a shramana did not feel.

He was open to everything that these people came to him with. He welcomed the merchant who had linen on offer, the debtor who was looking for a loan, the beggar who spent an hour recounting the story of his poverty and who was not half as poor as any shramana. Rich foreign merchants he treated no differently than the servant who shaved him or the street vendor whom he allowed to cheat him out of a few small coins when he bought bananas. When Kamaswami came to him to complain about his troubles or to take him to task over some business deal, he would listen with good humor and interest, marveling over him, trying to understand him. He would allow him to think he was right to the extent that he seemed to require and then would move on to the next person who sought his attention. And many people came to him. Many came to do business with him, to cheat him; many came to question him; many came to make a claim on his compassion, many to get his advice. He gave advice, sympathized with people, gave gifts, he let himself be cheated a little, and the whole game—and the passion with which people played the game—occupied his thoughts just as much as the gods and Brahman once had.

Now and then he sensed, deep in his breast, a faint, moribund voice, which faintly warned, softly complained—he could barely hear it. Then one day it came to his mind that he was leading a strange life, that the things he was occupied with were purely a game, that though he was in a cheerful frame of mind and sometimes felt happy, real life was passing him by without touching him. He was playing with his business dealings the way a juggler plays with balls; in the same way he played with the people around him, watched them, was amused by them. But he was not present to all this with his heart, with the wellspring of his being. That spring was running somewhere far away, running on unseen, and had nothing to do with his life anymore. More than once he recoiled from these thoughts, wishing it were possible for him to take part wholeheartedly and enthusiastically in the childish goings-on of everyday life, to be able really to live, really to act, really to enjoy life instead of merely being an observer watching it go by.

But he kept coming back to beautiful Kamala. He learned the art of love, practiced the rites of pleasure, in which—more than anywhere else—giving and taking became one. He prattled with her, learned from her, gave and received advice. She understood him better than Govinda ever had. She was more like him.

One day he said to her: "You are like me; you are different from most people. You are Kamala, no one else, and within you there is a stillness, a haven to which you can withdraw at any time and be at home there—just as I can. Few people have that, but yet all of them could have it."

"Not all people are smart," said Kamala.

"No," said Siddhartha, "it does not depend on that. Kamaswami is as smart as I am, and yet he has no haven within him. Others do have it who are mere children as far as their understanding goes. Most people, Kamala, are like fallen leaves that blow and whirl about in the air, then dip and fall to earth. But others, only a few, are like stars, which move on a fixed course where no wind reaches them; they have their law and their course within them. Among all the scholars and shramanas, of whom I know so many, there was one who was perfect in this sense. I can never forget him. That was Gotama, the Exalted One, the expounder of the teaching. Thousands of disciples listen to his teaching every day, follow his precepts hour by hour, but they are all falling leaves. They do not contain the law and the teaching within themselves."

Kamala regarded him with a smile. "Again you are

talking about him," she said. "Once again you are thinking shramana thoughts."

Siddhartha stopped talking and they played a game
of love, one of the thirty or forty games that Kamala
knew. Her body was pliant like that of a jaguar or like a
hunter's bow. Whoever was her student in love became
acquainted with many pleasures and many secrets. Long
she played the game with Siddhartha, seducing him,
denying him, taking him by force, engulfing him in her
embrace, enjoying her mastery, until he was subdued
and exhausted and resting at her side.

The courtesan bent over him, looked long into his
face and into his now-tired eyes.

"You are the best lover I have ever encountered," she
said thoughtfully. "You are stronger than the others,
more supple, more willing. You have learned my art
well, Siddhartha. Some day, when I am older, I would
like to have a child of yours. But in spite of all that, my
dear, you have remained a shramana and you do not
love me. You love no one, is that not so?"

"That may well be," Siddhartha said tiredly. "I am
like you. You too do not love; otherwise how could you
practice love as an art? People of our type are perhaps
incapable of love. The child people are capable of it;
that is their secret."

Samsara

For a long time Siddhartha lived the worldly life, the life of pleasure, without ever becoming a part of it. His senses, which he had mortified in his fervent shramana years, had reawakened. He had tasted wealth, pleasure, and power. Nevertheless, in his heart he long remained a shramana. Clever Kamala had been accurate in this. It was still the art of thinking, waiting, and fasting that guided his life. Worldly people, the child people, remained alien to him and he to them.

Years passed. Wrapped in life's comforts, Siddhartha hardly felt them go. He had become rich. He had long possessed his own house and servants as well as a garden on the city's edge, on the river. People liked him. They came to him when they needed money or advice, but no one was close to him apart from Kamala.

The sublime, brilliant wakefulness he had once known—in the prime of his youth, in the days following Gotama's discourse, following the separation from Govinda—that taut expectancy, that proud independence beyond learning and doctrine, that adaptable readiness to hear the divine voice in his own heart, had gradually become a memory, something transient. Remote and faint ran the sacred spring to which he had once been near, which had once run within himself. True, much that he had learned from the shramanas, from Gotama, from his father the brahmin, remained within him for a long time—moderation in life, pleasure in thought, the habit of meditation, intimate knowledge of the self, of the eternal self that is neither body nor consciousness. Much of that had remained in him, but one after the other those things had sunk from view and become covered with dust. Like a potter's wheel, which once set in motion continues to turn for a long time, only slowly losing momentum and winding down, in Siddhartha's soul the wheel of asceticism, the wheel of thinking, the wheel of discrimination, continued to turn for a long time. In fact that wheel was still turning, but slowly and haltingly, and was close to stopping. Slowly, as when moisture forces its way into a dying tree trunk, gradually filling it and causing it to rot, worldliness and lethargy were pushing into Siddhartha's soul, slowly filling it, making it heavy and tired, reducing it to torpor. On the other hand, his senses had come alive and were learning and experiencing a great deal.

Siddhartha had learned to do business, exercise power over people, take pleasure with women; he had learned to wear beautiful clothes, to command servants, and to bathe in perfumed water. He had learned to eat delicately and painstakingly prepared dishes—including fish, meat, and fowl, spices and sweets—and to drink the wine that leads to lethargy and oblivion. He had learned to play dice and chess, to have women

dance for him, to have himself carried in a litter, and to
sleep in a soft bed. But nonetheless he had continued to
feel different from the others and superior to them. He
had always looked at them with a touch of disdain, with
a touch of disdainful contempt, with just that contempt
that a shramana always feels toward worldly people.
Whenever Kamaswami was peevish, irritable, when he
took umbrage, was plagued by his businessman's worries, Siddhartha had always looked on him with disdain. Only gradually and imperceptibly, with the
passing of harvests and rainy seasons, did his disdain
begin to slacken and his sense of superiority begin to
become quiescent. Only gradually, amid his increasing
riches, did Siddhartha himself take on something of the
qualities of the child people, something of their childishness and fear. And yet he still envied them the one
thing he still lacked and they possessed—the sense of
importance they were able to attach to their lives, the
ardor of their joys and fears, the timorous but sweet
happiness of their eternal passion. These people were
perpetually in love with themselves, with women, with
their children, with honor or money, with their plans
and hopes. But just this one thing he was not able to
learn from them—this childlike joy and childish foolishness. He assimilated from them just the unpleasant
side, what he himself had contempt for. He began ever
more often, on mornings following an evening with
people, to stay in bed for a long time feeling stupid and
spent. He began to be irritable and impatient when
Kamaswami bored him with his troubles. He began to

laugh overloud when he lost at dice. His face was still more intelligent and more spiritual than others', but it seldom laughed and it took on one after another those qualities one finds so often in the faces of the rich—discontent, petulance, ill temper, lethargy, lovelessness. Gradually the soul sickness of the rich was taking him over.

Like a veil, like a thin mist, fatigue settled over Siddhartha, slowly, each day a bit thicker, each month a bit drearier, each year a bit heavier. As a new garment gets old with time, loses its vivid color, gets spotted, wrinkled, worn at the seams, and here and there begins to show weak, threadbare spots, in the same way Siddhartha's new life, which he had begun after his separation from Govinda, had grown old with the passing years and lost its color and luster, accumulated spots and wrinkles; and here and there, already poking through in an ugly fashion, waited the disappointment and revulsion that lay hidden beneath. Siddhartha failed to see it. He noticed only that the bright and confident voice of his inner being, which had once been awake within him and which in his times of brilliance had been his constant guide, had gone still.

The world had caught him—pleasure, greed, and indifference—and finally even the vice that he had always despised and derided as the most foolish of all, craving for possessions. Property—possessions and wealth—had finally also snared him. That, too, for him was no longer a game over empty trifles but had become a weight and chain. By a strange and devious route,

Siddhartha had fallen into the ultimate and most despicable of addictions—playing dice. From the time he ceased in his heart to be a shramana, Siddhartha began to gamble for money and precious objects with ever increasing zeal and passion. This was something he had formerly done lightheartedly and with a smile, just going along with a pastime of the child people. Now he was a feared player; he bet so high and brashly that few dared play with him. He gambled out of an inner need—gambling away, frittering away, the miserable lucre brought him a malicious pleasure. This way he could display his contempt for wealth and for the indulgences of the merchants in the plainest and most scornful way. So he played for high stakes, ruthlessly, hating himself, mocking himself. He raked in thousands, threw thousands away, gambled away money, jewelry, a country villa; then again he won and again he lost. He loved the fear, the dread and uncanny fear he felt throwing the dice with big stakes hanging in the balance, and he sought to reproduce it again and again, to intensify it further, to tease it to a higher level, for in this feeling alone he felt something like happiness, something like rapture, something like a heightened sense of life in the midst of his sated, lukewarm, stale existence. And after each large loss, he set his mind on new wealth, pushed harder in his business, exacted payment from debtors more sternly, for he wanted to gamble more, waste more; once more he wanted to show wealth his contempt. Siddhartha lost his equanimity toward losses, lost his patience with people slow to pay, lost his kindliness with beggars, lost his pleasure in giving gifts and lending money to those who asked for it. The same man who gambled away ten thousands on a throw of the dice and laughed became ever more exacting and mean in business, and even occasionally dreamed at night of money! And every time he awoke from this ugly spell, every time he saw his face in the mirror on his bedroom wall, changed by age and grown ugly, every time shame and revulsion came over him, he escaped further and harder, escaped into another gambling session, escaped into the oblivion of pleasure and wine and from there back into the preoccupations of amassing and gaining wealth. He drove himself on and on in this meaningless cycle until he was tired, until he was old, until he was sick.

Once he received a warning in a dream. He had spent the evening with Kamala, in her beautiful pleasure garden. They had sat beneath the trees talking, and Kamala had spoken pensive words veiling sadness and fatigue. She had asked him to tell her about Gotama and could not get her fill of hearing about him, how pure his gaze was, how still and beautiful his mouth, how kindly his smile, how tranquil his walk. He had to go on for a long time telling her stories about the venerable Buddha, and Kamala had sighed and said: "One day, perhaps soon, I shall follow this Buddha. I shall make him a gift of my pleasure garden and take refuge in his teaching." But then she had aroused him physically and in their lovemaking had locked him to her in painful throes of lust accompanied by biting and tears, as though she were trying to squeeze the last sweet drops out of vain, impermanent pleasure. Never was it clearer to Siddhartha how closely related love's pleasure is to death. Then he lay by Kamala's side with her face close to his, and around her eyes and the corners of her mouth he read plainly as never before a timid script, a script of fine lines and faint furrows, a script that recalled autumn and old age and also reminded Siddhartha of himself. He was in his forties now, and had here and there noticed gray hairs among the black. Fatigue was written on Kamala's beautiful face, the fatigue of a long journey that has no happy destination, fatigue and a suggestion of fading, and also a concealed, not-yet-expressed, perhaps not-yet-conscious alarm: fear of old age, fear of autumn, fear of having to die. Sighing, he had bid her farewell, his soul filled with malaise and hidden fear.

Then Siddhartha had spent the night in the company of dancing girls, drinking wine. He had played the superior among his peers, which he no longer was, had drunk a great deal of wine, and had gone to bed late, after midnight, tired and yet agitated, close to crying and despair. He had tried in vain to sleep, his heart filled with a misery he felt he could no longer bear, filled with a revulsion by which he felt totally saturated, as by the lukewarm, revolting taste of the wine, the cloying, meaningless music, the excessive smiles of the dancing girls, and the overly sweet odor of their hair and breasts. But above all he felt revulsion toward himself, his perfumed hair, the winy smell of his mouth, the loose tiredness and slackness of his skin. As when someone who has eaten and drunk too much goes through intense pain to vomit it back up but is still glad of the relief, thus the sleepless man, in a great flood of revulsion, longed to be rid of these pleasures, these habits, this whole meaningless life and himself altogether. Only by the morning light, with the first stirring of activity on the street, did he fall asleep and find for a few moments a partial deadening, a shred of sleep. In those few moments, he had a dream:

In a golden cage Kamala had a small, rare songbird. He dreamed about the bird. He dreamed the bird, who otherwise always sang in the morning, was silent. Noticing this, he went over to the cage and looked inside. The little bird was dead and lay stiff on the bottom of the cage. He took it out, weighed it a moment in his hand, then threw it away onto the street outside. That moment a terrible fright took hold of him and his heart pained him as though with this dead bird he had thrown away everything valuable and good.

Waking suddenly from this dream, he was enveloped in profound sadness. It was all worthless! It seemed to him that he had led his life in a worthless and meaningless way. He was left with nothing alive, nothing in any way precious or worth holding on to. He was alone and destitute, like a shipwreck victim cast up on the shore.

In a grim state, Siddhartha entered a pleasure garden that belonged to him, locked the gate, sat down beneath a mango tree, felt death in his heart and horror in his breast. He sat there and felt himself dying inside, withering, coming to an end. Little by little he gathered his thoughts and passed in his mind through the whole of his life, beginning with the earliest days he could recall. When had he experienced happiness, felt true bliss? Oh yes, he had experienced that more than once. He had tasted it in his boyhood when he had received praise from the brahmins, when, far in advance of the other boys of his age, he had distinguished himself in the recitation of the holy verses, in debate with the scholars, or as an assistant in the sacrifices. Then he had felt in his heart: "A path lies before you that you have been called to follow; the gods await you." And then again as a youth, as the goal of all thought, constantly slipping away from him upward, beyond his reach, drew him out of the multitude of his peers and ever upward toward itself: As he struggled painfully to seize the meaning of Brahman, as any knowledge he attained only aroused a further thirst—there again, in the middle of that thirst, in the midst of the pain, he had felt it again: "Onward! Onward! You have been called!" He had heard that voice when he had left his home, having chosen the life of the shramanas; and again, when he left the shramanas to go to the Perfect One; and also when he left him to push on into the unknown. How long had it been since he had heard that voice, how long since he had attained some height? How flat and desolate his path had become! Many a long year without a high aim, without inner thirst, without anything elevated—contented with little pleasures but still never satisfied! All these years, without realizing it, he had worked longingly toward becoming a person like all the others, like these children, and as he had pursued this, his life had become more miserable and poorer than theirs, for their goals and cares were not his. This whole world of Kamaswami people had after all only been a game for him, a dance that one watches, a show. Kamala was the only one he cared about and who was worth something to him. But was she still? Did he still need her, or she him? Were they not playing a game that had no end? Was it necessary to go on living for that? No, it was not necessary! The name of this game was samsara, a game for children, a game worth playing perhaps once, twice, ten times—but worth continuing to play forever?

Then Siddhartha knew that the game was over, that he could not play anymore. A shudder went over his body, through his insides, and he felt that something had died.

That whole day he sat under the mango tree, thinking about his father, about Govinda, about Gotama. Had it been necessary for him to leave them and become a Kamaswami? He was still sitting there when night fell. As he looked up and saw the stars, he thought: Here I sit in my pleasure garden under my mango tree. He smiled slightly—was it necessary, was it right, was it not a foolish game, that he owned a mango tree, a garden?

That, too, he put an end to, that died in him. He got to his feet, took his leave of the mango tree and the garden. Since he had been without food the whole day, he was very hungry and thought of his house in the city, of his bedchamber and his bed, of the table with food on it. With a tired smile, he shook himself and said good-bye to these things.

That very hour of that night, Siddhartha left his garden, left the city, never to return. Kamaswami had people out looking for him for a long time. He believed he had been the victim of bandits. Kamala sent no one to search for him. When she learned that Siddhartha had disappeared, it did not surprise her. Had she not always expected this? Was he not a shramana, a homeless one, a wayfarer? And she had felt this most deeply the last time she had been with him, and she rejoiced amid the pain of her loss that that last time she had drawn him so fervently to her bosom and had once more felt so completely possessed and penetrated by him.

When she first received news of Siddhartha's disappearance, she went to the window where she kept a rare songbird in a golden cage. She opened the door of the cage, took the bird out, and let it fly away. She looked after the flying bird for a long time. From that day, she stopped receiving visitors and kept her house closed. But after a time she became aware that, from her last time together with Siddhartha, she was pregnant.

By the River

SIDDHARTHA WANDERED in the forest. He was already far from the city. He knew only one thing—that he could not go back, that the life he had led for many years was over and gone. He had sucked it and drained it to the point of revulsion. The songbird of his dream was dead. The bird in his heart was dead. He was profoundly enmeshed in samsara. He had sucked nausea and death into himself from every side, as a sponge sucks up water until it is full. He was bloated with excess, with misery, with death. There was nothing left in the world that could attract him, nothing that could bring him pleasure or console him.

He earnestly wished to know no more of himself, to have quiet, to be dead. Let a thunderbolt come and strike him dead! Let a tiger come and devour him! Let there just be a wine, a poison, that would bring him numbness, oblivion, and sleep with no more awakening! Was there any sort of dirt left with which he had not dirtied himself, any sin or folly that he had not committed, any desolation of the soul that he had not brought upon himself? Was it still possible to live? Was it possible to draw breath and expel breath again and again, feel hunger and eat again, sleep again, lie with a woman again? Had he not exhausted this cycle of existence and come to the end of it?

Siddhartha arrived at the large river in the forest, the same river across which a ferryman had taken him when he was still a young man and was coming from the city of Gotama. At this river he stopped and remained standing hesitantly on the bank. He was weakened by fatigue and hunger, and what reason did he have to go on, where was he going, what was his goal? No, there was no goal anymore, there was nothing left but a profound, painful longing to shake off this whole vile dream, to spew out this stale wine, to make an end to this wretched and disgraceful life.

A tree grew bent over the river bank, a coconut tree. Siddhartha leaned his shoulder against it, laid his arm over the trunk, and gazed down into the green water that flowed endlessly by, gazed down and found himself wholly and completely filled with the desire to be rid of himself and sink beneath this water. A ghastly emptiness reflected back to him out of this water, which gave an answer to the terrible emptiness in his soul. Yes, he had reached the end. There was nothing left for him to do but extinguish himself, to smash the ruined figure of his life, to throw it away at the feet of the sneering gods. This was the great retching he longed for: death, the shattering of the form he hated! Let the fish eat him, this dog Siddhartha, this madman, this spoiled and rotten body, this flagging, abused soul! Let the fish and crocodiles devour him, let the demons tear him to pieces!

His face contorted, he stared into the water. He saw the reflection of his face and spat at it. Profoundly weary, he slipped his arm from the tree trunk and turned a little to allow himself to fall straight down, so he could go under at last. He sank, his eyes closed, toward death.

Just then, from remote precincts of his soul, out of one of the pasts of his outworn life, came a sound. It was a word, a syllable, which he began to mumble mindlessly, the old word from the beginning and end of every brahmanic prayer, the sacred OM, which means something like "perfection" or "fulfillment." And the moment the sound of OM reached Siddhartha's ear, suddenly his slumbering mind awakened, and he recognized the foolishness of his action.

Fear struck deep into Siddhartha. So this was the way things stood with him! He was so lost, so confused and forsaken by all wisdom that he had been able to seek death. His wish, the wish he had had as a child to find peace, had grown so large he had sought it in the dissolution of his body. That which all the pain—all the disillusionment and despair—of his recent life had not achieved had been brought about by the moment in which OM penetrated his awareness: He recognized himself in the midst of his misery and delusion.

"OM!" he said to himself, "OM!" And he knew Brahman, realized the indestructibility of life, recognized once again the dimension of divinity he had forgotten.

But this was just a moment, a flash. Siddhartha sank

down at the foot of the coconut tree, laid his head on its root, and sank into a deep sleep.

His sleep was deep and dreamless. It had been a long time since he had had such a sleep. When he awoke after many hours, it was as though ten years had passed. He heard the soft rushing of the water and did not know where he was, who had brought him to this place. He opened his eyes and looked with amazement at the trees and sky above him. The past seemed veiled, infinitely far away, remote, infinitely unimportant. He only knew that he had abandoned his earlier life (in that first moment of thought this earlier life struck him as some long-ago former incarnation, like a previous birth of his present ego). He knew that he had abandoned that earlier life, that he had been so filled with misery and revulsion that he had wanted to throw his life away, but that by a river, under a coconut tree, he had come to himself with the sacred word om on his lips, then had fallen asleep. Now, having reawakened, he looked at the world as a new man. Softly he uttered the word om, which he had fallen asleep saying, and it seemed to him that his whole long sleep had been nothing else but a long, fully absorbed recitation of om, a thinking of om, a submersion and a total entry into om, into the nameless, the perfect.

What a wonderful sleep this had been! Never had sleeping so refreshed, renewed, and rejuvenated him. Perhaps he had actually died, had gone under and been reborn in a new form? But no, he knew himself, he knew his hands and his feet, knew the place where he lay, knew this ego in his breast, this self-willed, odd person Siddhartha. But this Siddhartha was changed, renewed. He was remarkably well rested, remarkably alert, cheerful, and inquisitive.

Siddhartha sat up and saw a stranger near him, a monk in a yellow robe with shaved head, sitting in the posture of contemplation. He looked at the man, who had no hair on head or face, and he was not looking long before he recognized in this monk Govinda, the friend of his youth, who had taken refuge with the exalted Buddha. Govinda had aged too, but his face still bore the same traits, which expressed enthusiasm, loyalty, inquisitiveness, fearfulness. But now as Govinda, feeling his gaze, opened his eyes and looked at him, Siddhartha saw that Govinda did not recognize him. Govinda was happy to find him awake. Evidently he had been sitting there a long time waiting for him to wake up, even though he did not know him.

"I was asleep," said Siddhartha. "How did you happen to come here?"

"You were asleep," answered Govinda. "It is not good to sleep in such places, frequented by snakes and beasts of the wood. I, lord, am a disciple of exalted Gotama the Buddha, called Shakyamuni. I was passing this way with a number of our people when I saw you lying and sleeping in a place dangerous to sleep in. So I tried to wake you up, lord, but when I saw that you were sleeping very deeply, I let my people go on and remained behind sitting with you. And then, so it seems, I who meant to watch over your sleep, fell asleep myself. I performed my task badly; fatigue overcame me. But now that you are awake, let me go, so I can catch up with my brothers."

"Thank you, shramana, for guarding my sleep," Siddhartha said. "You disciples of the Exalted One are kind. Now you may go."

"I am going, lord. May goodness ever follow you."

"Thank you, shramana."

Govinda raised his hand in the sign of parting and said, "Farewell."

"Farewell, Govinda," Siddhartha said.

The monk stopped.

"With your permission, lord, how do you know my name?"

Siddhartha smiled.

"I know you, Govinda, from the hut of your father, from the brahmins' school, from the sacrifices, from the journey we took going after the shramanas, and from that time in the Jeta Grove when you took refuge with the Exalted One."

"You are Siddhartha!" Govinda loudly exclaimed. "Now I recognize you and cannot understand how I could have failed to recognize you right away. Welcome, Siddhartha. Great is my joy to see you again."

"I am glad to see you again too. You were the guardian of my sleep. I thank you for that again, though I had no need of a guardian. Where are you going, my friend?"

"I am going nowhere. We monks are always on the

move unless it is the rainy season. We continually travel from place to place, living according to our rule, proclaiming the teaching, collecting alms, moving on. It is always that way. But you, Siddhartha, where are you going?"

Siddhartha said: "It is the same with me, friend, as with you. I am going nowhere. I am just on the way, a wayfarer, a wanderer."

Govinda said: "You say you are a wanderer, and I believe you. But pardon me, Siddhartha, you do not look like a wanderer. You are wearing a rich man's garment, the shoes of a grandee, and your hair, which smells of perfume, is not the hair of a wanderer, of a shramana."

"Your sharp eyes see all, my friend. But I did not tell you I was a shramana. I just said I am a wanderer. And so it is: I am a wanderer."

"You are a wanderer," said Govinda. "But there are few wanderers who wander in such clothing, with such shoes, with such hair. Never, in my many years as a wanderer, have I met such a wanderer."

"I believe you, Govinda. But now, today, you have met such a wanderer, with such shoes and in such a garment. Remember, friend: Impermanent is the world of forms; clothing is impermanent—highly impermanent—along with the style of our hair, our hair itself, and our very bodies. I wear the clothing of a rich man, you saw aright. I wear it because I was a rich man, and I wear my hair as people of the world do, seekers after pleasure, for I was one myself."

"And now, Siddhartha, what are you now?"

"I do not know, any more than you do. I am on the way. I was a rich man and am one no longer. What I will be tomorrow, I do not know."

"You lost your wealth?"

"I lost it, or it me. It got away from me. The wheel of forms turns swiftly, Govinda. Where is the brahmin Siddhartha? Where is the shramana Siddhartha? Where is the rich man Siddhartha? That which is impermanent changes swiftly, as you know, Govinda."

Govinda looked at the friend of his youth for a long time with doubt in his eye. Then he took leave of him as one takes leave of a prominent person and went on his way.

Siddhartha looked after him, a smile on his face. He still loved him, this loyal, fearful person. And how would it have been possible not to love anybody or anything at this moment, in this glorious time after his wonderful sleep pervaded by OM! That was precisely the magic that had been worked in him by OM during his sleep—that he loved everything, that he was filled with joyous love of everything he saw. And precisely that was the reason, so it seemed to him now, that he had been so very sick before—because he had been unable to love anything or anybody.

With a smile on his face, Siddhartha watched the monk disappear. His sleep had strengthened him a great deal, but he was acutely tormented by hunger, for he had not eaten for two days, and the time was long in the past when he had been inured to hunger. With grief but also humor, he thought about those times. Then, as he recalled, he had boasted to Kamala of three things, that he had mastered three noble and invincible arts: fasting, waiting, and thinking. This had been his wealth, his power and strength, his trusty staff; in the diligent, hardworking years of his youth he had learned these three skills—nothing else. And now they had abandoned him, none of them belonged to him anymore—neither fasting, nor waiting, nor thinking. He had given them away in exchange for the most miserable pittance, the most impermanent of things: sensual pleasure, comfort, and wealth! Strange but true, this is how it had been. And now, it seemed to him, he had actually become one of the child people.

Siddhartha reflected on his situation. It was hard for him to think—basically he had no taste for it—but he forced himself.

Now, he thought, since all these highly impermanent things have gotten away from me, I stand once again under the sun as I stood as a child—I have nothing, I know nothing, I have no abilities, I have learned nothing. How strange! Now that I am no longer young, my hair is half gray, and my powers are on the wane, I am starting all over from the beginning like a child! He had to smile again. Yes, his fate was strange! He had come down in the world, and now here he was again, empty and naked and ignorant. But he could feel no sorrow over this; no, he even felt a strong impulse to laugh, laugh about himself, laugh about this strange, foolish world.

"You are going down!" he said to himself and laughed. And as he said it, his eyes fell on the river, and he saw the river was going down too, flowing ever downward, and singing happily as it did. He liked that a lot. He gave the river a friendly smile. Was this not the river he had once intended to drown himself in, a hundred years ago, or had he only dreamed that?

My life has been strange indeed, he thought to himself; it has taken strange twists and turns. As a boy, I was totally involved with gods and sacrifices. As a youth, I was completely occupied with asceticism, thinking, and meditating; I was searching for Brahman and I worshiped the eternal in the atman. As a young man, I followed the ascetics, lived in the forest, suffered heat and frost, learned to go hungry, taught my body how to wither. Then miraculously knowledge came to me in the teaching of the great Buddha, and I felt the realization of the unity of the world circulating in me like my own blood. But I also had to leave the Buddha and that great wisdom behind. I went and learned from Kamala the pleasures of love, learned business from Kamaswami, accumulated money, frittered money away, learned to love my stomach, learned to indulge my senses. It took me many years of that to lose my connection with mind, to lose the ability to think, to forget unity. Is it not true that slowly and by long circuitous ways I changed from a man to a child, from a thinker to one of the child people? But still this journey was good, and still the bird in my breast did not die. But what a journey that was! I had to pass through so much ignorance, so much vice, such great misunderstanding, so much revulsion and disappointment and misery—just to become a child again and start over. But it was right. My heart affirms it. My eyes laugh upon it. I had to experience despair, I had to sink to the level of the stupidest of all thoughts, the thought of suicide, in order to be able to experience grace, to hear OM again, to sleep properly again and be able to awaken properly. I had to become a fool to find atman in myself again. I had to sin to be able to live again. Where can my way lead now? It is a foolish way, one has to drag oneself along it; maybe it is circular. But let it be as it pleases, I will follow it.

He felt a wonderful surge of joy within him.

"Where," he asked his heart, "are you getting this happiness from? Is it really coming from that long, good sleep that did me so much good? Or is it from the word OM that I uttered? Or does it come from the fact that I have skipped out, I have made good my escape, I am finally free again like a child under the sky? Oh, how good it is to have gotten away, to be free! How pure and beautiful the air is here, how good to breathe! There, in the place I ran away from, everything smelled of unguents, spices, wine, excess, lethargy. How I hated that world of rich men, gluttons, and gamblers! How I hated myself for staying so long in that horrific world! How I hated myself, robbed myself, poisoned myself, tormented myself, made myself into someone old and nasty! No, never again will I imagine, as I used to do so readily, that Siddhartha is wise! But one thing I have done that is good, that pleases me, that I find laud-able—I have now put an end to that self-hatred and that foolish, empty life. Praise be to you, Siddhartha, after so many years of stupidity, you have once again had an idea, you have done something. You heard the bird in your breast singing and you followed it!"

Thus he praised himself, rejoiced in himself, and lis-tened to his stomach with curiosity as it growled with hunger. He felt that in the last period, over the last days, he had fully chewed and thoroughly tasted a great mass of suffering, a great chunk of misery, and spit it out. He had devoured every last bit of it, to the point of de-spair and death. This was good. He might have stayed a lot longer with Kamaswami, making and squandering money, stuffing his belly and letting his soul die of thirst. He might have lived a lot longer in that soft, well-upholstered hell, if one thing had not come about—the moment of total hopelessness and despair, that mo-ment of final extremity when he hung over the rushing water and was ready to destroy himself. That he had felt that despair, that profoundest revulsion, and had not been broken by it, that the bird, that wellspring, that happy voice, was still alive in him—that is where his joy came from. That is why he was laughing; that is why his face was radiant beneath his graying hair.

It is good, he thought, to experience directly for one-self what one has to understand. I already understood as a child that the pleasures of the world and wealth are not good things. I understood that long ago, but I have only just now experienced it. And now I know it, not only from memory but with my eyes, my heart, my stomach. Good for me for knowing it!

He reflected for a long time on his transformation, listened to the bird sing with joy. Had this bird within him not died? Had he not felt its death? No, something else in him had died, something that had been longing to die for a long time. Was it not the same thing he had wanted to exterminate in his ardent years as an ascetic? Was it not his ego, his little, fearful, and prideful ego, against which he had fought for so many years, but which had conquered him again, which was there again after every extermination, banishing joy and feeling fear? Was it not this that finally today had died, here in the forest by this lovely river? Was it not because of this death that he was now like a child, so full of confidence, so fearless, so full of joy?

Now Siddhartha also knew why, as a brahmin and an ascetic, his fight against this ego had been futile. Too much knowledge had held him back, too many sacred verses, too many ritual rules, too much denial, too much doing and striving. He had been full of arrogance—always the smartest, always the most industrious, always a step ahead of everybody, always wise and spiritual, always the priest or sage. Into this priesthood, into this high-mindedness, into this spirituality, his ego had crept. It had anchored itself there and grown even as he thought he was destroying it through fasting and austerities. Now he saw it, and saw that the secret voice had been right. No teacher could ever have saved him. That is why he had had to go into the world and abandon himself to pleasure and power, women and money, why he had had to be a merchant, a dice player, a drinker, and a man consumed with greed—until the priest and shramana within him were dead. That is why he had to continue to endure these ugly years, to endure the revulsion, the emptiness, the meaninglessness of a lost and desolate life until the end, to the point of bitter despair, until Siddhartha the hedonist, Siddhartha the greedy, could die. He had died and a new Siddhartha had awakened from his sleep. He too would get old and would have to die. Siddhartha was impermanent, every formed thing was impermanent. But today he was young, a child, the new Siddhartha, and full of joy.

He thought these thoughts, listened with a smile to his stomach, heard with gratitude a buzzing bee. Cheerfully, he looked into the flowing river. Never had he liked water as much as in this river. Never had he perceived the sound and image of moving water as so vivid and beautiful. It seemed to him that the river had something special to tell him, something he did not yet know, that still lay ahead of him. In this river Siddhartha had wanted to drown himself; in it today, the old, tired, despairing Siddhartha had drowned. But the new Siddhartha felt a profound love toward this flowing stream and resolved not to leave it soon.

The Ferryman

I WILL STAY by this river, Siddhartha thought. It is
the same one I crossed long ago on the way to the
child people. A kindly ferryman took me across then. I
will go to him. My way to a new life once started at his
hut. That life is now old and dead. May my new way, my
new life, have its starting point there!

Tenderly he gazed into the translucent greenness of
the flowing water, at the crystalline lines of the mysterious designs it made. He saw pale pearls rising out of the
depths and still bubbles floating on the surface with the
image of the blue sky in them. The river looked at him
with a thousand eyes, green ones, white ones, crystal
ones, sky blue ones. How he loved this river, how it
charmed him, how grateful he was to it! In his heart he
heard the voice speaking, the newly awakened voice,
and it said to him: "Love this river! Stay by it! Learn
from it!" Oh yes, he wanted to learn from it, to listen to
it. Whoever could understand this river and its mysteries, it seemed to him, would also understand many
other things, many mysteries, all mysteries.

Among the mysteries of the river today, however, he
saw only one that gripped his soul. He saw that the river

flowed and flowed, flowed ever onward, and yet was always there, was always the same yet every moment new! Oh, if one could grasp that, understand that! He did not understand or grasp it, felt only an inkling stir, a distant memory, divine voices.

Siddhartha got up. The stabs of hunger in his body had become unbearable. Driven by them, he wandered up the path on the riverbank, upriver. He listened to the current, listened to the snarling of hunger in his gut.

When he reached the place where the ferry crossed, the boat lay at the ready, and the same ferryman who had once taken the young shramana across the river stood in the boat. Siddhartha recognized him—he too had greatly aged.

"Will you take me across?" he asked.

The ferryman, astonished to see such an eminent person wandering alone and on foot, took him into the boat and pushed off.

"You have chosen a wonderful life," said the guest. "It must be wonderful to live every day on this river and ply its waters."

Smiling, the oarsman swayed back and forth. "It is wonderful, lord, as you say. But is not every life, every task, wonderful?"

"That may be. However, I envy you yours."

"Ach, you might soon get tired of it. It is not something for people in fine clothes."

Siddhartha laughed. "Already once today I have been judged by my clothes, suspiciously. Will you not, ferryman, accept from me these clothes, which have become a burden to me? For you should know that I have no money to pay you the price of the crossing."

"The lord is joking," laughed the ferryman.

"I am not joking, my friend. Listen, once before you took me across this river in your boat for nothing more than the gratitude of the gods. Do that again today, and accept my clothing for it as well."

"And does the lord intend to continue his travels without any clothes?"

"Actually I would prefer not to continue my travels at all. What I would most like, ferryman, is if you would give me an old tunic and keep me with you as your helper, or rather as your apprentice, for to begin with I will have to learn how to work with the boat."

The ferryman gave the stranger a long and searching look.

"Now I recognize you," he said at last. "Once you slept in my hut, a long time ago now, perhaps more than twenty years ago; and I took you across the river and we parted from each other good friends. Were you not a shramana? I cannot any longer recall your name."

"My name is Siddhartha, and I was a shramana when you last saw me."

"Then you are welcome, Siddhartha. My name is Vasudeva. I hope you will be my guest again today and sleep in my hut and tell me where you come from and why your beautiful clothes are such a burden to you."

They had reached the middle of the river, and Vasudeva leaned harder on his oar in order to make headway against the current. He worked calmly with his powerful arms, his eye on the prow of the boat. Siddhartha sat and watched him and recalled how, long ago, in the last days of his time as a shramana, love for this man had arisen in his heart. With gratitude he accepted Vasudeva's invitation. When they came alongside the bank, he helped him tie up the boat at its mooring. Then the ferryman asked him to come into the hut and offered him bread and water, which Siddhartha ate with pleasure, as well as the mangos that Vasudeva offered him.

Afterward—it was getting on toward sunset—they sat down on a tree trunk on the bank, and Siddhartha told the ferryman about his origins and about his life as he had seen it pass before his eyes that day during his hour of despair. His tale lasted deep into the night.

Vasudeva listened with great attention. As he listened, he took everything in, origins and childhood, all the studying, the seeking, all the joys, all the troubles. Of the ferryman's virtues, this was one of his greatest: He knew how to listen as few people do. Though Vasudeva spoke not a word himself, the speaker felt him receiving his words into himself, quietly, openly, unhurriedly, missing nothing, not jumping ahead through impatience, attributing neither praise nor blame—just listening. Siddhartha felt what happiness can come from opening oneself to such a listener, having one's own life—one's seeking, one's suffering—enter this other's heart.

Toward the end of Siddhartha's story, as he was talking about the tree by the river, of how low he had fallen, of the sacred OM, and what deep love he had felt for the river after his sleep, the ferryman listened with attention redoubled, fully and completely given over, his eyes closed.

When Siddhartha had stopped talking and after the long silence that followed had passed, Vasudeva said: "It is as I thought. The river spoke to you. It is your friend too; it speaks to you too. That is good; that is very good. Stay with me, Siddhartha, my friend. Once I had a wife. Her bed was next to mine, but she died long ago. I have lived by myself for a long time. Live with me now. There is room and food for both of us.

"Thank you," said Siddhartha. "I thank you and accept. And I also thank you, Vasudeva, for having listened to me so well! Few people know how to listen, and I never met anyone who knows how as well as you. In this, too, I will learn from you."

"You will learn that," said Vasudeva, "but not from me. The river taught me how to listen; you will learn that from the river too. The river knows everything; everything can be learned from it. Look, you have already learned from the river that it is good to aim low, to sink, to seek the bottom. The rich and prominent Siddhartha has become an oarsman's helper; this, too, was the advice of the river. You will learn the other thing from it too."

After a long pause, Siddhartha said: "What is the other thing, Vasudeva?"

Vasudeva got up. "It is late," he said. "Let us go to sleep. I cannot tell you what the other thing is, my friend. You will learn it. Perhaps you know it already. Look, I am no scholar. I do not know how to talk and I also do not know how to think. I only know how to listen and how to be respectful. I have not learned anything else. If I could express that and teach it, perhaps I would be a wise man. But as it is, I am only a ferryman, and my task is to take people across this river. I have taken many across, thousands, and for all of them my river has been nothing but an obstacle on their journey. They were traveling for money and business, to weddings, on pilgrimages, and the river was in their way. The ferryman was there to take them quickly past the obstacle. For a few among the thousands—very few, four or five of them—the river stopped being an obstacle. They heard its voice, they listened to it, and the river became sacred to them as it has to me. Let us now take our rest, Siddhartha."

Siddhartha stayed with the ferryman and learned the work of the boat. And when there was nothing to do on the ferry, he worked with Vasudeva in the rice field, gathered wood, picked fruit from the banana tree. He learned how to make an oar, repair the boat, weave baskets, and was glad about everything he learned. And the days and months passed swiftly by. But the river taught him more than Vasudeva could. He learned from it unceasingly. Above all he learned from it how to listen, how to listen with a still heart, with an expectant, open soul, without passion, without desire, without judgment, without opinion.

He and Vasudeva lived together in friendship, and

from time to time they exchanged words—few words long pondered. Vasudeva was no friend of words. Siddhartha seldom succeeded in getting him to talk.

Once he asked him: "Have you also learned from the river the secret that there is no time?"

A bright smile came over Vasudeva's face. "Yes, Siddhartha," he said. "This is probably what you mean: that the river is everywhere at once—at its source, at its mouth, by the waterfall, by the ferry crossing, in the rapids, in the sea, in the mountains—everywhere at the same time. And that for it there is only the present, not the shadow called the future."

"That's it," said Siddhartha. "And when I learned that, I looked at my life, and it too was a river; and the boy Siddhartha and the man Siddhartha and the old man Siddhartha were only separated by shadows, not by anything real. Siddhartha's previous births were also not a past, and his death and return to Brahma were not a future. Nothing was, nothing will be; everything is, everything has its being and is present."

Siddhartha spoke with rapture; this revelation had brought him profound happiness. Was not all suffering time, was not all self-torment and fearfulness time? Was not all that was heavy and hostile in the world overcome and over with once one had overcome time, had been able to rid oneself of the notion of time? He had spoken with rapture. But Vasudeva only smiled at him radiantly and nodded confirmation. Silently he nodded, stroked Siddhartha's shoulder with his hand, and returned to his work.

And another time, in the rainy season when the river was swollen and rushing headlong, Siddhartha said: "Is it not true, friend, that the river has many voices, very many voices? Does it not have the voice of a king, of a warrior, of a bull, of a night bird, of a woman giving birth, of a man sighing, and a thousand other voices too?"

"That is true," nodded Vasudeva, "all creatures' voices are in its voice."

"And do you know," Siddhartha continued, "what word it speaks when you succeed in hearing all its ten thousand voices at once?"

Happiness shone in Vasudeva's face as he laughed. He leaned over to Siddhartha and whispered the sacred OM into his ear. And that is just what Siddhartha had also heard.

And from one occasion to the next, his smile came more and more to resemble the ferryman's. It became nearly as radiant, nearly as aglow with happiness, shone in the same way out of a thousand little wrinkles, was just as much like a child's and just as much like an old man's. Many travelers, seeing the two ferrymen, took them for brothers. Often the two sat in the evening on the tree trunk on the bank and listened in silence to the river, which for them was not a river but the voice of life, the voice of what is, eternal becoming. And occasionally it happened that while listening to the river both men would think of the same thing—a conversation from the day before yesterday, one of their passengers whose face and fortune had caught their interest, of death, of their childhood; and then at the same moment, when the river had said something good to them, they would look at each other, both thinking exactly the same thing, both gladdened by the same answer to the same question.

Something emanated from the ferry and the two ferrymen that was sensed by many of the travelers. It sometimes happened that a traveler, after looking into the face of one of the ferrymen, began to tell the story of his life, recounted his suffering, confessed evil, and asked for consolation and advice. It happened occasionally that one of the travelers asked for permission to stay for an evening and listen to the river. It also came to pass that curiosity seekers came who had been told that two wise men or magicians or saints lived at the ferry crossing. The curiosity seekers asked many questions, but they got no answers, and they found neither magicians nor wise men. They found only two old and kindly little men, who seemed to be mute and a bit odd and dotty. And the curiosity seekers laughed and had conversations about how foolish and gullible people were to spread such empty rumors.

Years went by with nobody counting them. Once monks came wandering who were followers of Gotama the Buddha. They asked to be taken across the river, and from them the ferrymen learned that they were going with all speed back to see their great teacher, for the word had spread that the Exalted One was mortally ill and would soon die his last death as a human and enter the state of liberation. Not long after, another large group of monks came and then another, and the monks as well as most of the other travelers and wanderers spoke of nothing but Gotama and his impending death. As to a crusade or a king's coronation, people streamed from everywhere, from all directions, gathering in swarms like ants and streaming onward as though compelled by magic toward the place where the great Buddha was awaiting death, where that enormity was to occur, where the Perfect One of the age was to enter into glory.

Siddhartha thought a great deal during this time about the dying sage, the great teacher whose voice had counseled nations and awakened hundreds of thousands of people, whose voice he too had heard once, whose holy countenance he too had looked upon with awe. Warmly he thought of him, saw the teacher's path to perfection before his eyes, and remembered with a smile the words that once, as a young man, he had addressed to the Exalted One. It seemed to him they had been proud and precocious words; smiling, he recalled them. For a long time he had known himself to be no longer separate from Gotama, whose teaching nevertheless he had been unable to accept. No, a true seeker, one who truly wished to find, could not accept any doctrine. But he who had found realization could look with favor on any teaching, any path, any goal. Nothing any longer separated him from a thousand others who lived the eternal, who breathed the divine.

On one of those days when so many people were making their pilgrimage to the dying Buddha, Kamala, once the most beautiful of courtesans, appeared among them. She had long since withdrawn from her former life, had made a gift of her garden to the monks of Gotama, had taken refuge in the teaching, and was among the friends and benefactors of those traveling to see the Buddha. Along with the boy Siddhartha, her son, she had begun her journey as soon as she had heard of the Buddha's imminent death. She wore a simple garment and was traveling on foot. With her little son she was traveling along the river, but the boy would tire quickly and would want to go back home. He wanted to rest, he wanted to eat. He would become quarrelsome and whiny. Kamala had to make frequent rest stops with him. He was accustomed to imposing his will on hers. She had to feed him, console him, scold him. He did not understand why he had to go with his mother on this toilsome and sad journey to an unknown place to see a man he did not know, a man who was holy and lay dying. Let him die, what did the boy care?

Those two travelers were not far from Vasudeva's ferry crossing when the little Siddhartha prevailed upon his mother to stop for a rest. Kamala was also tired, and while the child chewed on a banana, she squatted on the ground, closing her eyes a little to rest. But then she suddenly emitted a loud wail. The boy looked at her in terror and saw her face go gray with shock. From beneath Kamala's dress the small black snake escaped that had bitten her.

Now the two ran hurriedly down the path trying to reach some people. They reached the vicinity of the ferry crossing, and there Kamala collapsed, unable to go farther. The boy began screaming pitifully. Between screams he kissed his mother and threw his arms around her neck. She added her voice to his loud cries for help, and the sounds reached the ears of Vasudeva, who was standing by the ferry. He came quickly, took the woman in his arms, and carried her onto the boat, with the boy at his heels. Soon the three arrived at the hut, where Siddhartha was at the hearth making a fire. He looked up and saw first the face of the boy, which oddly jolted his memory, reminding him of something forgotten. Then he saw Kamala, whom he recognized immediately although she lay unconscious in the ferryman's arms; and now he knew that it was his own son whose face had so startled his memory, and his heart was moved within him.

Kamala's wound was washed, but it was already black and her body was swollen. A healing drink was given to her, and her consciousness returned. She lay on Siddhartha's bed in the hut, and Siddhartha, who had once loved her so dearly, bent over her. She thought she was dreaming. Smiling, she gazed at her friend's face. Only slowly did she piece the situation together. She remembered the snakebite and cried out anxiously for the boy.

"He is near, do not worry," said Siddhartha.

Kamala looked into his eyes. She spoke with a heavy tongue, numbed by the poison. "You have grown old, my love," she said. "You have gone gray. But you resemble the young shramana who once came to me in the garden without clothes and with dusty feet. You resemble him a lot more than you did at the time you left me and Kamaswami. In your eyes, you resemble him, Siddhartha. Oh, I too have grown old, old. Did you still know me, Siddhartha?"

Siddhartha smiled. "I knew you immediately, Kamala, my love."

Kamala pointed to the boy and said, "Did you know him, too? He is your son."

Her eyes lost focus and fell shut. The boy cried. Siddhartha took him on his knee, let him cry, stroked his hair. The look of his child's face recalled to him a brahmanic prayer, which he had learned long ago when he was a child. He began to chant it in singsong tones. The words flowed to him out of the past, from his childhood. Under the spell of the chant, the boy calmed down, shook with a few more sobs, and fell asleep. Siddhartha laid him on Vasudeva's bed. Vasudeva was standing by the hearth cooking rice. Siddhartha gave him a look, which he returned smiling.

"She is going to die," said Siddhartha softly.

Vasudeva nodded. The light of the flames in the hearth played over his kindly face.

Kamala came to again. Pain distorted her face. Siddhartha's eyes read the suffering in her mouth, in her blanched cheeks. He noted it quietly, attentively, patiently, absorbed in her suffering. Kamala felt this and her eyes sought his.

Gazing at him, she said, "Now I see that your eyes have also changed. They have become quite different.

So how can I still recognize you as Siddhartha? You are him and you are not."

Siddhartha did not speak. In silence he gazed into her eyes.

"You achieved it?" she asked. "You found peace?"

He smiled and laid his hand on hers.

"I see it," she said, "I see it. I too will find peace."

"You have found it," whispered Siddhartha.

Kamala looked steadily into his eyes. She thought about her intention to go to see Gotama. She had wanted to see the face of one who had achieved perfection, to breathe in his peacefulness. She thought that instead of him she had now found Siddhartha and that this was good, just as good as if she had seen Gotama. She wanted to say this, but her tongue no longer obeyed her will. In silence she looked at him, and he saw the life going out of her eyes. The last pain filled her eyes and broke, and as the last shudder ran over her limbs, his fingers closed her eyelids.

Long he sat and looked at her dead face. For a long time he looked at her mouth, her old tired mouth with its shrunken lips, and he remembered that once in the springtime of his years he had compared that mouth to a fig freshly broken open. He sat for a long time contemplating the pallid face, the tired wrinkles, filling himself with the sight. He saw his own face reposing that way, just as white, just as lifeless; and at the same time he saw his face and her face when young, with the red lips, the burning eyes; and the feeling of presence and simultaneity pervaded him completely, a feeling of eternity. He felt profoundly at that moment, more profoundly than ever, the indestructibility of life, the eternity of every instant.

By the time he got up, Vasudeva had prepared him some rice. But Siddhartha did not eat. In the goat stall, the two old men made a bed of straw, and Vasudeva lay down to sleep. But Siddhartha went out and sat in front of the hut through the night, listening to the river, his past washing over him, touched and surrounded by all the periods of his life at the same time.

Early in the morning, before the sun became visible, Vasudeva came out of the stall and approached his friend.

"You did not sleep," he said.

"No, Vasudeva. I sat here and listened to the river. It told me a lot. It filled me deeply with healing thoughts, thoughts of unity."

"You experienced pain, Siddhartha, but I see that no sadness has entered your heart."

"No, dear friend, why should I be sad? I who was once rich and happy have become still richer and happier. I have received the gift of my son."

"Your son is welcome as far as I am concerned too. But now, Siddhartha, let us get to work. There is plenty to do. Kamala has died in the same bed my wife once died in. We should build Kamala's pyre on the same hill where I once built my wife's pyre."

While the boy still slept, they built the funeral pyre.

The Son

Sʜʏ ᴀɴᴅ ᴄʀʏɪɴɢ, the boy stood by at his mother's last rites. Gloomy and shy, he listened to Siddhartha greet him as his son and tell him he was welcome to stay with him in Vasudeva's hut. Pale, he sat whole days on the funeral hill. He would not eat. He averted his gaze and closed his heart, pushing away his fate, trying to defy it.

Siddhartha was easy on him and let him have his way. He honored his mourning. Siddhartha understood that his son did not know him, that he could not love him as a father. Gradually he saw and also understood that the eleven-year-old was a spoiled boy, a mother's child, used to fine food, a soft bed, in the habit of giving orders to servants. Siddhartha understood that the grieving and spoiled child could not all at once accept this strangeness and poverty with good cheer. He did not force him. He did much of his work for him, always sought out for him the best bits of food. He hoped slowly to win him over through kindness and patience.

He had proclaimed himself rich and happy when the boy had come to him. But as time went by and the boy remained aloof and morose, showed a proud and obstinate heart, was unwilling to do any work, showed the old men no respect, and poached from Vasudeva's fruit trees, Siddhartha began to understand that with his son it was not happiness and peace that had come to him, but suffering and trouble. But he loved him and preferred the suffering and trouble of love to happiness and joy without the boy.

From the time the young Siddhartha was with them in the hut, the old men began dividing the work between them. Vasudeva once more took over the ferry work on his own, and Siddhartha, in order to remain near his son, did the work in the hut and the field.

For a long time, long months, Siddhartha waited for his son to understand him, to accept his love and perhaps return it. For long months Vasudeva waited, observing. He waited and said nothing. One day when the young Siddhartha had again been rudely tormenting his father with his obstinacy and moodiness and had broken two rice bowls, Vasudeva took his friend aside in the evening and spoke with him.

"Excuse me," he said, "I want to speak to you in all friendship. I see that you are torturing yourself, I see that you are troubled. Your son, my friend, causes you grief, and he causes me grief too. The young bird is used to another life, another kind of nest. He has not, like you, run away from wealth and the city out of revulsion and a sense of excess. He had to leave all that behind against his will. I have asked the river, my friend, many times I have asked it. But the river laughs, he laughs at me, he laughs at you and me; he shakes with laughter over our foolishness. Water seeks water, youth seeks youth. Your son is not in a place where he can flourish. You ask the river yourself, you listen to it too!"

Troubled, Siddhartha looked into the kindly face, in whose many wrinkles dwelled constant cheerfulness.

"Can I part with him?" he asked softly, ashamed. "Give me time, my friend! Do you not see: I am struggling with him, I am trying to win his heart. I am trying to capture it through love and friendly patience. The river will one day speak to him too. He too has been called."

Vasudeva's smile shone still more warmly. "Oh yes, he too has been called; he too is part of eternal life. But do we know, you and I, to what he has been called, to what paths, to what deeds, to what suffering? His suffering will not be slight, for his heart is proud and hard. Such people must suffer much, stray far, commit much wrongdoing, weigh themselves down with many sins. Tell me, my friend, is it not true that you do not give your son any training? You do not force him to do anything? You do not beat him? You do not punish him?"

"No, Vasudeva, I do not do any of those things."

"I knew it. You do not force him, beat him, or give him any orders, because you know that soft is stronger than hard, water stronger than rock, love stronger than force. Very good. You have my praise. But is it not a mistake on your part to think that you are not forcing him and not punishing him? Are you not binding him with the bonds of your love? Do you not shame him every day and do you not make things still harder for him through your kindness and patience? Are you not forcing him, this high-strung and spoiled boy, to live in a hut with two old banana munchers, for whom rice is already a delicacy, whose thoughts could not be his, whose hearts are old and at peace and move at a different pace from his? Is all that not force and a punishment?"

Shocked, Siddhartha looked down at the ground. "What do you think I should do?" he asked softly.

Vasudeva said: "Bring him to the city, bring him to his mother's house. There will still be servants there. Give him to them. And if they are not there anymore, then take him to a teacher—not for the sake of the teacher, but so he will be with other boys and girls and in the world that is his. Have you never thought of that?"

"You see into my heart," Siddhartha said sadly. "I have often thought of it. But look, how can I abandon the boy, whose heart is already not a gentle one, to this world? Will he not indulge himself in luxury, get lost in pleasure and power? Will he not repeat all of his father's mistakes? Will he not perhaps get completely lost in samsara?"

The ferryman smiled brightly. He touched Siddhartha tenderly on the arm and said: "Ask the river about it, my friend! Listen to him laugh about it! Do you really believe you committed your follies so you could save your son from them? Can you protect your son from samsara? How could you? Through teaching, through prayer, through warnings? My dear friend, have you completely forgotten the instructive story of the brahmin's son Siddhartha that you once told me on this very spot? Who saved the shramana Siddhartha from samsara, from sin, from greed, from foolishness? Were his father's piety, his teacher's warnings, his own knowledge, or his seeking mind able to save him? What father or teacher could have shielded him from living life himself, from soiling himself with life, from blaming himself, from drinking the bitter potion himself, from finding his way on his own? Do you, my friend, believe that perhaps someone could be spared having to tread this path? Perhaps your little son, because you love him, because you would so much like to spare him suffering and pain and disappointment? But even if you were to die for him ten times over, you would not be able to subtract the tiniest fragment from his fate."

Never before had Vasudeva said so many words. Siddhartha thanked him warmly and returned to the hut in distress. For a long time he could not sleep. Vasudeva had not told him anything he had not already thought and known himself. But this was knowledge he could not put into action. His love for the child, his tenderness, and his fear of losing him were stronger than his knowledge. Had he ever lost his heart so completely to anything? Had he ever loved anyone this way, so blindly, so painfully, so unsuccessfully, and yet with such happiness?

Siddhartha could not follow his friend's advice. He was unable to give up his son. He let himself be ordered around by the boy; he let himself be disregarded by him. He said nothing and waited, undertook anew each day the struggle of kindness, the silent war of patience. Vasudeva also said nothing and waited, was friendly, understanding, and forbearing. In matters of patience, they were both masters.

Once, at a moment when the boy's face strongly reminded him of Kamala, Siddhartha found himself suddenly considering something Kamala had said to him many years ago in the time of their youth. "You are incapable of love," she had said to him, and he had agreed with her and had compared himself to a star and the child people to falling leaves. Nevertheless he had felt the reproach in her words. It was true, he had never been able to lose himself entirely in another person, never been able to give himself completely. Never had he been able to forget himself and become love's fool for another. His inability to do that, as it seemed to him in those days, was the main thing that separated him from the child people. But now, since his son had been with him, Siddhartha, too, had become altogether one of the child people, suffering for another person, loving another person, lost in love, a fool for love. Now, belatedly, he too felt, for the first time in his life, this strangest and strongest passion. He suffered from it, suffered pitifully, but was nevertheless touched by bliss, was in some way renewed and in some way richer.

Of course he was aware that this love, this blind love for his son, was a passion, something very human, samsara. He was aware that it was a wellspring of troubled, murky waters. But at the same time he felt it was not worthless—it was something necessary, arising from his own being. This appetite, too, wanted to be experienced and redeemed; this folly, too, had to be committed.

The son for his part allowed him to commit his follies, let him try to win him over, let him continue to undergo the daily discouragement brought on by the boy's moods. There was nothing about this father that either charmed him or instilled fear in him. This father was a good man, a good, kind, gentle man, maybe a very pious man, maybe a saint. But none of these were qualities that were winning ones for the boy. He was bored with this father, who held him captive in his miserable hut. He was bored with him for meeting his every nasty trick with a smile, his every insult with kindness, his every act of malice with goodness. Just that was the most hated thing in the old fraud's bag of tricks. The boy would have much preferred to be threatened and treated badly by him.

A day came when young Siddhartha's resentment finally erupted into open defiance of his father. His father had given him a task; he had told him to gather some brushwood. But the boy did not leave the hut. He stood there obstinate and enraged, stamped on the floor, curled his hands into fists, and in a violent outburst of hatred and contempt, shouted into his father's face.

"Get your own brushwood!" he cried, spitting with fury. "I'm not a servant. Yes, it's true you do not beat me—because you do not dare! What you do is constantly try to demean me and punish me with your piety and kindness. You want me to become like you, just as pious, just as gentle, just as wise! But hear me:

To your sorrow, I would rather be a bandit and a murderer and go to hell than be like you! I hate you! You are not my father, even if you were my mother's lover ten times over!"

Anger and resentment toward his father poured out of him in a stream of vile and evil words. Then the boy ran off and did not return until late in the evening.

And on the following morning he was gone. Also gone was a small basket woven from two-colored hemp in which the ferrymen kept the copper and silver coins they received as payment for the ferry. The boat was gone too. Siddhartha saw it on the other bank. The boy had run away.

"I must follow him," said Siddhartha, who had been trembling with hurt since the boy's abusive speech of the day before. "The child cannot get through the forest on his own. He will die. We must build a raft, Vasudeva, to get to the other side."

"We shall build a raft," said Vasudeva, "in order to get our boat back, which the boy made off with. But him, my friend, you should let go. He is no longer a child. He knows how to take care of himself. He is looking for the road back to the city, and he is right—do not forget that. He is doing what you yourself fell short of doing. He is shifting for himself, he is going his way. Oh, Siddhartha, I see you are suffering, but you are suffering pains that might be worth laughing over. You will soon be laughing over them yourself."

Siddhartha did not answer. He already had the axe in

his hand and was beginning to make a raft out of bamboo. Vasudeva helped him to bind the stalks together with grass cord. Then they floated across, were carried far downstream, and had to tow the raft upstream again along the opposite shore.

"Why did you bring the axe along?" asked Siddhartha.

Vasudeva said: "It could be our boat's oar has been lost."

But Siddhartha knew what his friend was thinking. He was thinking the boy had probably thrown the oar away or broken it, out of revenge and to slow their pursuit. And in truth there was no oar in the boat. Vasudeva pointed to the bottom of the boat and looked at his friend with a smile, as if to say: "Do you not see, my friend, what your son is trying to tell us? Do you not see that he does not want to be followed?" But he did not put this into words. He began making a new oar. Siddhartha, however, took his leave so he could look for the runaway. Vasudeva did not hold him back.

Siddhartha had already been traveling through the forest a long time when he was struck by the idea that his search was futile. Either the boy is far ahead of me, he thought, and has already reached the city; or if he is still on the way, he will stay hidden from his pursuer. As he thought further, he realized also that he was not worried about his son. Deep inside he knew the boy had not died and also that the forest did not represent a dangerous threat to him. Nevertheless he kept walking without stopping for a rest, no longer in order to save him, but just perhaps to see him once more. And he walked till he reached the outskirts of the city.

When he came to where the road widens near the city, he stopped at the entrance to the pleasure garden that had once belonged to Kamala, the place where long ago he had seen her in her litter for the first time. That past time came to life in his mind, and he saw himself standing there again, young, a naked, bearded shramana, his hair full of dust. Siddhartha stood there for a long time looking through the gate into the garden. He saw monks in yellow robes walking beneath the lovely trees.

He stood for a long time thinking, seeing images, caught up in the story of his life. He stood for a long time watching the monks, and in their stead he saw the young Siddhartha and the young Kamala walking beneath the tall trees. Clearly he saw himself being received by Kamala and getting his first kiss from her, saw himself looking back on his brahmin's life with pride and disdain and, full of desire, beginning his life in the world. He saw Kamaswami, the servants, the feasting, the dice-playing, the musicians, and he saw Kamala's songbird in its cage. He lived through all these things again, breathed in samsara, became old and tired again, felt again the revulsion, felt again the desire to put an end to himself, and healed once again through the sacred OM.

After he had stood a long time at the garden gate, Siddhartha realized that the longing that had driven him to this place was a foolish one, that he could not help his son, that he ought not to cling to him. In his heart he felt deeply his love for the runaway. He felt it like a wound, and at the same time he felt he had been given the wound not so he could wallow in the pain of it but so it could become a flower, a shining blossom.

It made him sad that at this moment the wound was not yet a blossom, was not yet shining. In the place of the wishful thinking that had drawn him to this place in pursuit of his runaway son, there was now emptiness. Sadly, he sat down, felt something in his heart die, felt the emptiness, felt no joy, saw no point. He sat absorbed and waited. This he had learned by the river, this one thing—to wait, have patience, listen. And he sat in the dust of the road and listened, listened to his heart sadly and tiredly beating, waited for his voice. For many hours he squatted there listening, seeing no more images, sinking into emptiness, letting himself sink, seeing no road ahead. And when he felt the wound burning, he uttered the OM soundlessly, filled himself with OM. The monks in the garden saw him. After he had squatted there for many hours with the dust gathering in his hair, one of them came and laid two bananas on the ground in front of him. The old man did not see him.

He was awakened from this fixed state by a hand touching his shoulder. He immediately recognized this tender and modest touch, and came to himself. He stood up and greeted Vasudeva, who had followed him. And as he looked into Vasudeva's face, at the little wrinkles filled with a pure smiling quality, into the cheerful eyes, he too smiled. He now saw the bananas that lay before him, picked them up, gave one to the ferryman, and ate the other himself. Then he went in silence back into the forest with Vasudeva and returned to his home at the ferry. Neither of them spoke of the day's happenings, neither spoke the boy's name nor mentioned his flight. Neither spoke of the wound. In the hut, Siddhartha lay on his bed, and a little while later when Vasudeva came to him with a bowl of coconut milk, he found him already asleep.

Om

THE WOUND continued to burn for a long time. Siddhartha had to take many travelers across the river who had a son or a daughter with them, and he never laid his eyes on one of them without feeling envy, without thinking: "So many people, so many thousands, possess this most wonderful of happinesses, why not I? Bad people, even thieves and bandits, have children, love them, and are loved by them in return, only not me." So simple were his thoughts now, so without understanding. That is how much he had come to resemble the child people.

Now he looked at people differently than he had before—less cleverly, with less pride, yet more warmly, with more curiosity and caring. When he took travelers of the usual kind across the river, child people—traders, warriors, women—these people no longer seemed alien to him, as they once had. He understood them, he shared their life, a life guided not by ideas and insights but only by impulses and desires. He felt as they did. Although he was nearer to perfection and bore his last wound, it nevertheless seemed to him that these people were his brothers. Their vanities, appetites, and absurd traits had lost their absurdity for him. These traits had become comprehensible, lovable; he even experienced them as worthy of respect. The blind love of a mother for her child, the ignorant, blind pride of a conceited father over his only little son, the raw hunger of vain, young women for jewelry and the admiring looks of men—all these impulses, all these childish qualities, all these simple and foolish but incredibly powerful, intensely vivid, forcefully dominant impulses and cravings were no longer childishness for Siddhartha. He saw that people live for them, achieve an endless amount for them, travel, wage war, suffer, and persevere unendingly for them. And he could love them for that. He saw life, that which is living, the indestructible essence, Brahman, in all of their passions, in each of their deeds. These people were worthy of love and admiration in their blind loyalty, in their blind strength and tenacity. There was nothing they lacked. The wise man and thinker had nothing over them except one trifle, one little tiny thing: the awareness, the conscious idea, of the unity of all life. And Siddhartha even doubted many a time that this knowledge, this idea, was so very valuable—was it not perhaps an example of the childishness of the think people, the intellectual version of the child people? The people of the world were the equals of the sages in all else, were often far superior to them, just as animals are often superior to human beings in their tough, unerring accomplishment of the necessary.

There slowly bloomed and ripened in Siddhartha the realization and knowledge of what wisdom, the object of his long quest, really was. It was nothing more than a readiness of the soul, a mysterious knack: the ability at every moment in the midst of life to think the thought of unity, to feel and breathe unity. Gradually this blossomed in him, shone back to him from the ancient child's face of Vasudeva—harmony, knowledge of the eternal perfection of the world, unity—a smile.

But the wound still burned. Passionately and bitterly, Siddhartha dwelled on his son, nurtured the love and tenderness in his heart, let the pain of it consume him, indulged in all the foolishness of love. This was not a flame that went out by itself.

One day when the wound was burning fiercely, Siddhartha crossed the river, driven by longing. He climbed out of the boat, intending to go to the city and look for his son. The river was flowing gently and quietly—it was the dry season. But there was something unusual about its voice. It was laughing, it was clearly laughing! The river was laughing, loudly and plainly laughing at the old ferryman. Siddhartha stopped, bent over the water to hear better, and in the quietly moving water he saw the reflection of his face. In this reflected face there was something that recalled something forgotten, and as he thought about it he remembered. This face was like another face he had once known and loved and also feared. It resembled the face of his father, the brahmin. And he remembered how, long ago as a youth, he had forced his father to let him go with the ascetics, how he had left him, gone off, and never returned. Had his father not felt the same pain over him that he now felt over his son? Had his father not long since died, alone, without ever having seen his son again? Should he not expect the same fate himself? Was it not comical, a strange and stupid thing, this repetition, this movement in the same fateful circles?

The river laughed. Yes, so it was. Everything returned that had not been suffered through to the end and resolved. The same pains were always suffered again. Siddhartha got back in the boat and rowed back to the hut, thinking of his father and of his son, with the river laughing at him, tending in his mind toward despair and tending not less toward joining in the laughter at himself and the whole world. The wound was not flowering yet, his heart was still fighting his fate, cheerfulness and victory had yet to shine forth from his chagrin. But he felt hope, and when he got back to the hut, he had an indomitable longing to open himself to Vasudeva, to expose everything to that master of listening, tell him everything.

Vasudeva was sitting in the hut weaving a basket. He no longer worked the boat. His eyes had begun to get weak, and his arms and hands too. All that remained unchanged, still glowing, was the joy and cheerful goodwill in his face.

Siddhartha sat down by the old man and slowly began talking. Things that they had never talked about, he talked about now: about the time he had gone back to the city, about the burning wound, about his jealousy when he saw happy fathers, about knowing better about such desires and yet struggling in vain against them. He described everything, he was able to say everything, even the most awkward things. He was able to say everything, expose everything, recount everything. He described his wound, told about the events of the day—how he had crossed the river like a runaway child, intending to go to the city, and how the river had laughed.

As he spoke—and he went on for a long time—Vasudeva listened to him with his face still, and Siddhartha felt more than ever the power of Vasudeva's listening. He felt his pains and anxieties going over to him, crossing over and coming back from the other side. Exposing his wound to this listener was the same as bathing it in the river, until it was cooled and became one with the water. As he went on speaking, continued to unbosom and confess himself, Siddhartha felt more and more that it was no longer Vasudeva, no longer a person, who was listening to him, that this unmoving listener soaking up his confession into himself as a tree draws in rain, this motionless being was the river itself, God himself, the eternal itself. And when Siddhartha stopped thinking about himself and his wound, the knowledge of Vasudeva's changed nature took possession of him; and the more he felt it and penetrated into it, the more wondrous it became, the more he realized that everything was in order, was natural; and he realized that Vasudeva had been that way for a long time, almost always—it was only he who had not completely recognized it; and yes, he realized that he himself hardly differed from Vasudeva anymore. He had the impression that he was now seeing old Vasudeva the way ordinary people see the gods—and that this was not something that could last. He began to take leave of Vasudeva in his heart. And all the while he went on talking.

When Siddhartha had talked himself out, Vasudeva turned his kindly, now weakened gaze on him and, without speaking, silently radiated love and cheerfulness to him, radiated understanding and wisdom. He took Siddhartha by the hand, led him to the seat on the riverbank, sat down with him at the river, smiling.

"You have heard him laugh," he said, "but you have not heard everything. Let us listen; you will hear more."

They listened. Softly came the many-voiced song of the river. Siddhartha looked into it, and in the moving water, images appeared to him. His father appeared, alone, mourning for his son. He himself appeared, alone, also tied with bonds of longing to his faraway son. His son appeared, alone too, lustily storming along the burning pathway of his youthful desires. Each was bent on his object, each possessed by his object; each suffered. The river sang with a voice of suffering; passionately it sang. Passionately it flowed toward its goal, its voice lamenting.

"Do you hear?" asked Vasudeva's mute glance. Siddhartha nodded.

"Listen closer," whispered Vasudeva.

Siddhartha made the effort to listen closer. The image of his father, his own image, and the image of his son flowed into one another. Kamala's image also appeared and dissolved. Govinda's image and other images appeared and fused with one another, and all became the river, all moved as the river toward their objects, their goals, passionate, hungering, suffering. And the river's voice was full of longing, ardent with sorrow, full of unquenchable longing. The river strove toward its goal; Siddhartha saw it hurrying on, this river composed of himself and those near him and of all the people he had ever seen. All the waves and currents hurried onward, suffering, toward objects, many goals. The waterfall, the lake, the rapids, the sea, and all the goals were reached; and each was followed by a new one, and the water became vapor and climbed into the sky, became rain and crashed down from the sky, became springs, brooks, became a river, strove onward again, flowed anew. But the passionate voice had changed. It still had the sound of suffering, questing, but other voices were added—voices of joy and suffering, good and evil voices, laughing and lamenting voices, a hundred, a thousand voices.

Siddhartha listened. He was now all listener, completely one with listening, completely empty, completely receptive. He felt now that he had completed his learning of how to listen. He had often heard all these things before, these many voices in the river, but today he heard it in a new way. Now he no longer distinguished the many voices, the happy from the grieving, the childlike from the manly. They were all part of each other— longing laments, the laughter of the wise, cries of anger, and the moans of the dying—all were one, all were interwoven and linked, intertwined in a thousand ways. And everything together, all the voices, all the goals, all the striving, all the suffering, all the pleasure—everything together was the river of what is, the music of life. And when Siddhartha listened attentively to the thousandfold song of the river, when he did not fasten on the suffering or the laughing, when he did not attach his mind to any one voice and become involved in it with his ego—when he listened to all of them, the whole, when he perceived the unity, then the great song of a thousand voices formed one single word: OM, perfection.

"Do you hear?" asked Vasudeva's eyes again.

Bright shone Vasudeva's smile; it hovered, glowing, in all the wrinkles of his aged countenance, just as the OM hovered over all the voices of the river. Bright shone his smile as he gazed at his friend, and now the same smile shone brightly in Siddhartha's face. His wound blossomed, his suffering was radiant, his ego had dissolved into the unity.

At this moment Siddhartha ceased to struggle with fate, ceased to suffer. On his face bloomed the cheerfulness of wisdom that is no longer opposed by will, that knows perfection, that is in harmony with the river of what is, with the current of life, full of compassion, full of empathic joy, surrendered to the flow, part of the unity.

As Vasudeva rose from the seat on the riverbank, as he looked into Siddhartha's eyes and saw the cheerfulness of wisdom radiant there, he touched his shoulder lightly with his hand in his considerate and tender way and said: "I have waited for this moment, dear friend. Now that it has come, let me go. I have long awaited this moment. I have long been the ferryman Vasudeva. Now it is enough. Farewell hut, farewell river, farewell Siddhartha!"

Siddhartha bowed low before the leave-taker.

"I knew it," he said softly. "You will go into the forest?"

"I am going into the forest. I am going into the unity," said Vasudeva, beaming.

Beaming, he went his way. Siddhartha looked after him. With profound joy and profound seriousness he looked after him, observed his tranquil walk, saw his countenance aglow, saw his form full of light.

Govinda

ONCE GOVINDA was passing his time during a rest period with the other monks in the pleasure garden that the courtesan Kamala had given to the disciples of Gotama. He heard talk of an old ferryman who lived a day's journey away on the river and was considered by many to be a sage. When Govinda resumed his wandering, he took the direction of the ferry, eager to see this ferryman. For though he had indeed lived his whole life according to the monastic rule and was looked upon by the younger monks with great respect on account of his age and humility, in his heart his restlessness and seeking had not been resolved.

He arrived at the river and asked the old man to take him across. As they were climbing out of the boat on the far side, he said to the old man: "You show much kindness to us monks and wanderers; you have taken many of us across the river. Are you not also, ferryman, a seeker of the true path?"

Smiling from his old eyes, Siddhartha said: "Do you call yourself a seeker, venerable one, though you are already advanced in years and wear the robe of the monks of Gotama?"

"It is true I am old," said Govinda, "but I have still not stopped seeking. I will never stop seeking—this seems to be my nature. You, too, as it seems to me, have also been a seeker. Will you not tell me something about it, your reverence?"

Siddhartha said: "What should I have to tell you, venerable one? Perhaps that you seek overmuch? That you seek so much you do not find?"

"How is that?" asked Govinda.

"When someone seeks," said Siddhartha, "it can easily happen that his eyes only see the thing he is seeking and that he is incapable of finding anything, incapable of taking anything in, because he is always only thinking about what he is seeking, because he has an object, a goal, because he is possessed by this goal. Seeking means having a goal, but finding means being free, open, having no goal. Perhaps you, venerable one, are indeed a seeker, for in striving after your goal, there is much you fail to see that is right before your eyes."

"I still do not entirely understand," said Govinda. "What do you mean by that?"

Siddhartha said: "Once, venerable one, many years ago, you came to this river, and by the river you found a man sleeping, and you sat by him in order to guard his sleep. But you did not recognize that sleeping man, Govinda."

Astonished, bedazzled, the monk looked into the ferryman's eyes.

"Are you Siddhartha?" he asked, his voice diffident. "I would not have recognized you this time either! I greet you warmly, Siddhartha; I am very happy to see you again. You have changed, my friend. So, you have now become a ferryman?"

Siddhartha laughed affectionately. "A ferryman, yes. Certain people, Govinda, must change a lot, must wear all kinds of outfits. I am one of those, dear friend. You are welcome, Govinda. Spend the night in my hut."

Govinda spent the night in the hut and slept on the bed that had once been Vasudeva's. He put many questions to the friend of his youth. Siddhartha had to recount much of his life.

The next morning, when it was time to begin the day's traveling, Govinda, not without hesitation, said these words: "Before I continue on my way, Siddhartha, allow me a question. Do you have a teaching? Do you have a belief or particular ideas that you follow that help you to live and act properly?"

Siddhartha said: "You know, friend, that already as a young man, in the days when we were living with the ascetics in the forest, I had come to mistrust teachers and teachings and had turned away from them. I stuck with that approach. Nevertheless, I have had many teachers since then. A beautiful courtesan was my teacher for a long time, and a rich merchant, and a few dice players. Once a wandering disciple of the Buddha was also my teacher. He sat with me in the course of his wanderings as I was sleeping in the forest. From him, too, I learned, and I am grateful to him, too, very grateful. But most of all, I have learned from this river here, and from my predecessor, the ferryman Vasudeva. He was a very simple man, Vasudeva. He was not a thinker, but he knew the essential just as well as Gotama. He was a perfect being, a saint."

Govinda said: "It seems to me, Siddhartha, that you still enjoy mocking me a little. I believe you and know you did not follow a teacher. But do you not have, if not a teaching, particular ideas, particular insights that you have come upon that are your own and that help you to live? If you would be so kind as to tell me something of these, it would gladden my heart."

Siddhartha said: "I have had ideas, yes, and insights too, all along. At times I have felt wisdom in me for an hour or for a day, just as a person will sometimes feel the life in his heart. There were many ideas, but it would be difficult for me to express them to you. See here, Govinda, this is one of the ideas that I have come to: Wisdom is not expressible. Wisdom, when a wise man tries to express it, always sounds like foolishness."

"Are you joking?" asked Govinda.

"I am not joking. I am telling you what I have discovered. Knowledge can be expressed, but not wisdom. One can discover it, one can live it, one can be borne along by it, one can do miracles with it, but one cannot express it and teach it. This is what I already sensed as a youth, what drove me away from teachers. I have come to an idea, Govinda, that you once more will take for a joke or some foolishness, but nevertheless it is my best idea. It is this: The opposite of every truth is also just as true! It is like this: A truth can be expressed and cloaked in words only if it is one-sided. Everything that can be thought in thoughts and expressed in words is one-sided, only a half. All such thoughts lack wholeness, fullness, unity. When the venerable Gotama taught and spoke of the world, he had to divide it into samsara and nirvana, deception and truth, suffering and liberation. There is no other possibility, no other way for those who would teach. But the world itself, existence around us and within us, is never one-sided. Never is a person or an act wholly samsara or wholly nirvana; never is a person entirely holy or sinful. That only appears to be the case because we are in the grips of the illusion that time is real. Time is not real, Govinda, I have experienced this many, many times. And if time is not real, then the gap that seems to exist between the world and eternity, between suffering and bliss, between good and evil, is also an illusion."

"How so?" asked Govinda uneasily.

"Listen well, friend, listen well! The sinner that I am and you are is indeed a sinner, but in time he will again be Brahma, in time he will attain nirvana, be a buddha. But see here, this 'in time' is an illusion, only a metaphor. The sinner is not on the path to buddhahood, he is not caught up in a process, even though our intellect knows no other way of representing things. No, the future buddha is present here and now within the sinner, his future is entirely there already. You must venerate the developing, potential, hidden buddha in him, in yourself, in everyone. The world, my friend Govinda, is not imperfect or confined at a point somewhere along a gradual pathway toward perfection. No, it is perfect at every moment. Every sin already contains grace within it, all little children already have an old person in them, every infant has death within it, and all dying people have within them eternal life. It is not possible for any person to see in another how far along the way he is. In the bandit and dice player a buddha is waiting; in the brahmin a bandit. In the depths of meditation lies the possibility of cutting through time, of seeing the simultaneity of all past, present, and future life, and that within that, everything is good, all is perfect, all is Brahman. Thus I see whatever is as good. I see that life and death, sin and holiness, intelligence and foolishness, must be as they are. It all only requires my consent, my willingness, my loving acceptance and it will be good for me, can never harm me. I have experienced in my own mind and body that I was very much in need of sin; I needed sensual pleasure, striving for possessions, vanity, and extreme debasement and despair in order to learn to give up resisting, in order to learn to love the world, in order to cease comparing it to some imagined world that I wished for, some form of perfection I had thought up, and let it be as it is and love it and be glad to be part of it.

"These, Govinda, are some of the ideas that have come to my mind."

Siddhartha bent over, picked up a stone off the ground, and weighed it in his hand.

"This," he said playfully, "is a stone, and after a certain length of time, it will perhaps be earth, and from the earth a plant will come, or an animal or a person.

Formerly I would have said: 'This is just a stone, it is worthless, part of the world of Maya. But in the cycle of transformations it can also become human and spirit, and so I attribute value to it.' That is perhaps how I used to think. But today I think: 'This stone is a stone, it is also a beast, it is also God, it is also Buddha.' I do not venerate and love it because someday it may become this or that but because it long since is and ever will be everything—and just on this account: that it is a stone, that it appears to me here and now as a stone—just because of that I love it and see value and meaning in its veins and pits, in its yellow, in its gray, in its hardness, in the sound it makes when I give it a knock, in the dryness or moistness of its surface. There are stones that feel like oil or soap, others that feel like leaves, others that feel like sand, and each one is unique and prays the OM in its own way. Each one is Brahman, but at the same time and just as much, it is a stone, oily or soapy—and just that is what pleases me and seems wonderful to me, worthy of veneration.

"But let me say no more. Words do no justice to the hidden meaning. Everything immediately becomes slightly different when it is expressed in words, a little bit distorted, a little foolish. And that too is good and pleases me very much. It is perfectly fine with me that what for one man is precious wisdom for another sounds like foolery."

Govinda listened to him without speaking. Then after a pause he asked hesitantly, "Why did you tell me that thing about the stone?"

"There was no particular purpose. Or perhaps I meant by it that I love the stone and the river and all these things that we look at and from which we can learn. I can love a stone, Govinda, and also a tree, or a piece of bark. Those are things, and a person can love things. But words I cannot love. That is why teachings are nothing for me. They have no hardness, no softness, no colors, no edges, no odor, no taste. They have nothing but words. Perhaps this is what prevents you from finding contentment—perhaps it is all the words. For *liberation* and *virtue* and *samsara* and *nirvana* are mere words, Govinda. There is no thing that is nirvana. There is only the word *nirvana*."

Govinda said: "Nirvana is not only a word, friend, it is an idea."

Siddhartha continued: "An idea it may be. But I must confess to you, my friend, I do not make a great distinction between ideas and words. Frankly, I do not have a high opinion of ideas either. I place more value on things. Here on this ferryboat, for example, I had a predecessor who was also my teacher, a holy man, who for many a long year simply believed in the river and nothing else. He noticed that the voice of the river spoke to him. He learned from it. That voice brought him up and taught him. For him the river was a god. For many years he did not know that every wind, cloud, bird, or beetle is equally divine and knows and can teach just as much as the venerable river. But by the time this sainted man went off into the forest, he knew everything, knew more than you and I—without a teacher, without books, just because he believed in the river."

Govinda said: "But is that which you call 'thing' something real, part of the essential nature of reality? Is it not only the deception of Maya, only image and appearance? Your stone, your tree, your river—are they truly realities?"

"This does not matter much to me either," said Siddhartha. "Let things be mere appearances or not—if so, I too am a mere appearance, and then they are still my fellows and peers. That is what makes them so dear and worthy of veneration: They are my equals. That is why I can love them. And here now is a teaching you will find laughable: Love, for me, Govinda, is clearly the main thing. Let seeing through the world, explaining it, looking down on it, be the business of great thinkers. The only thing of importance to me is being able to love the world, without looking down on it, without hating it and myself—being able to regard it and myself and all beings with love, admiration, and reverence."

"This I understand," said Govinda. "But this is just what the Exalted One recognized as a deception. He advocated goodwill, consideration, compassion, and tolerance, but not love. He forbade us to bind our hearts to anything earthly through love."

"I know," said Siddhartha; his smile was glowing like gold. "I know, Govinda. And with that we are smack in the middle of the jungle of opinions, disputing over words. For I cannot deny that my words about love contradict, or seemingly contradict, Gotama's words. That is just the reason I so mistrust words, for I know this contradiction is an illusion. I know that I am in agreement with Gotama. How is it possible that he would not know love? He saw the transitoriness and emptiness of human existence, and yet he so loved human beings that he spent the whole of his long life working hard to help them and teach them. In the case of your great teacher, too, the thing is preferable to the words, his actions and his life more important than his words, the gestures of his hand more important than his views. It is not in his speech and thought that I see his greatness, but only in his action, his life."

The two old men were silent for a long time. Then Govinda said, as he bowed his farewell: "Thank you, Siddhartha, for having told me something of your ideas. They are in part curious ideas; not all of them were immediately comprehensible for me. But be that as it may, I thank you and wish you days of peace."

(But secretly he thought to himself: This Siddhartha is a strange man, the ideas he expresses are strange, his teaching is so much foolishness. The pure teaching of the Exalted One is different—clearer, purer, more understandable. There is nothing in it that is bizarre, foolish, or preposterous. But Siddhartha's hands and feet, his eyes, his forehead, his breathing, his smile, his greeting, and his gait strike me entirely differently than his ideas. Never since our exalted Gotama entered nirvana have I encountered anyone of whom I felt: This is a saint! Only him, Siddhartha, has impressed me this way. Though his teaching is strange, though his words sound foolish, his gaze and his hand, his skin and his hair, everything about him radiates purity, calm, cheerfulness, moderation, and holiness. I have not seen anyone else like this since the death of our venerable teacher.)

As Govinda was thinking these thoughts, with conflicting impressions in his heart, he was drawn by love to bow to Siddhartha once again. Low he bowed before the man calmly sitting there.

"Siddhartha," he said, "we have become old men. It is unlikely that we will see each other in this body again. I see, my beloved friend, that you have found peace. I confess that I have not done so. Tell me a little more, revered one, give me something to take that I can grasp, that I can understand! Give me something to take with me on my way. My way is often onerous, Siddhartha, often grim."

Siddhartha remained silent and looked at him with his unchanging, quiet smile. Govinda looked into his face fixedly, with fear and longing. Suffering and perpetual seeking were written in his face, and perpetual failure to find.

Siddhartha saw this and smiled.

"Bend down to me!" he whispered softly in Govinda's ear. "Bend down to me! Closer! All the way! Kiss me on the forehead, Govinda!"

While Govinda, stunned but nevertheless magnetized by great love and anticipation, obeyed his words, bent over him, and touched his lips to his forehead, a marvelous thing happened to him. While his thoughts were still dwelling on Siddhartha's strange words, while he was still vainly and with some resistance attempting to think away time, mentally to represent nirvana and samsara as one, while indeed a certain disregard for his friend's words warred in him with inconceivable love and respect, the following thing happened to him:

He ceased to see his friend Siddhartha's face. In its stead he saw other faces, many, a long series, a flowing river of faces, hundreds, thousands, which all came and went, and yet all seemed to be there at once, which all constantly changed and became new ones, and yet were all Siddhartha. He saw the face of a fish, a carp, with its maw opened in limitless pain, a dying fish with bursting eyes. He saw the face of a newborn child, red and covered with wrinkles, distorted by crying. He saw the face of a murderer, saw him stick a knife into a person's body. In the same instant, he saw this criminal kneeling in chains and his head being cut off by an executioner with a sword. He saw the bodies of men and women naked in the postures and battles of ravenous lovemaking. He saw corpses stretched out—still, cold, vacant. He saw animal heads, heads of boars, crocodiles, elephants, bulls, and birds. He saw gods—Krishna and Agni. He saw all these forms and faces in a thousand relationships to one another, each helping the others, hating them, destroying them, giving birth to them again. Each was a death urge, a passionate and painful confession of impermanence, yet none died; each only transformed, was continually born anew, continually became a new face, yet without any time gap between one face and the other. And all these forms and faces rested, flowed, were begotten, floated onward, and flowed into one another. And over everything something thin, inessential yet existing, was continuously drawn, like thin glass or ice, like a transparent skin, a sheath or mold or mask of water. The mask was smiling, and the mask was Siddhartha's smiling face, which he, Govinda, was touching with his lips in this self-same instant. Thus Govinda saw the smile of the mask, the smile of unity over the flowing forms, the smile of simultaneity over the myriad births and deaths. This smile of Siddhartha's was exactly the same, resembled exactly the still, refined, impenetrable, perhaps-kind-perhaps-disdainful, wise, thousandfold smile of Gotama the Buddha, just as he himself, awestruck, had seen it a hundred times. So Govinda knew, this is the way the Perfect Ones smile.

No longer knowing if time existed, whether this vision had lasted a second or a hundred years, no longer knowing whether such a thing as a Siddhartha or a Gotama or an I-and-you existed, as though wounded at the quick by a divine arrow whose wound tasted sweet, befuddled and unstrung deep in his inmost being, Govinda remained bent over Siddhartha's still face—which he had just finished kissing, which had just been the scene of all form, all becoming, all being—for a little while longer. That countenance was unchanged, its surface having reclosed over the depths of thousandfold multiplicity. Siddhartha smiled quietly, smiled mildly and gently, perhaps with kindness, perhaps quite disdainfully, precisely as the Exalted One had smiled.

Govinda bowed low. Tears of which he was unaware ran down his aged face. A feeling of most profound love and most humble veneration burned like a fire in his heart. He bowed low, down to the ground, before the motionless, sitting figure whose smile reminded him of everything he had ever loved in his life, of everything in his life that had ever been worthy and sacred for him.

ABOUT THE AUTHOR

H ERMANN HESSE was born in 1877 in Calw, Germany. He was the son and grandson of Protestant missionaries and was educated in religious schools until the age of thirteen, when he dropped out of school. At age eighteen he moved to Basel, Switzerland, to work as a bookseller and lived in Switzerland for most of his life. His early novels included *Peter Camenzind* (1904), *Beneath the Wheel* (1906), *Gertrud* (1910), and *Rosshalde* (1914). During this period Hesse married and had three sons.

During World War I Hesse worked to supply German prisoners of war with reading materials and expressed his pacifist leanings in antiwar tracts and novels. Hesse's lifelong battles with depression drew him to study Freud during this period and, later, to undergo analysis with Jung. His first major literary success was the novel *Demian* (1919).

When Hesse's first marriage ended, he moved to Montagnola, Switzerland, where he created his best-known works: *Siddhartha* (1922), *Steppenwolf* (1927),

Narcissus and Goldmund (1930), *Journey to the East* (1932), and *The Glass Bead Game* (1943). Hesse won the Nobel Price for Literature in 1946. He died in 1962 at the age of eighty-five.